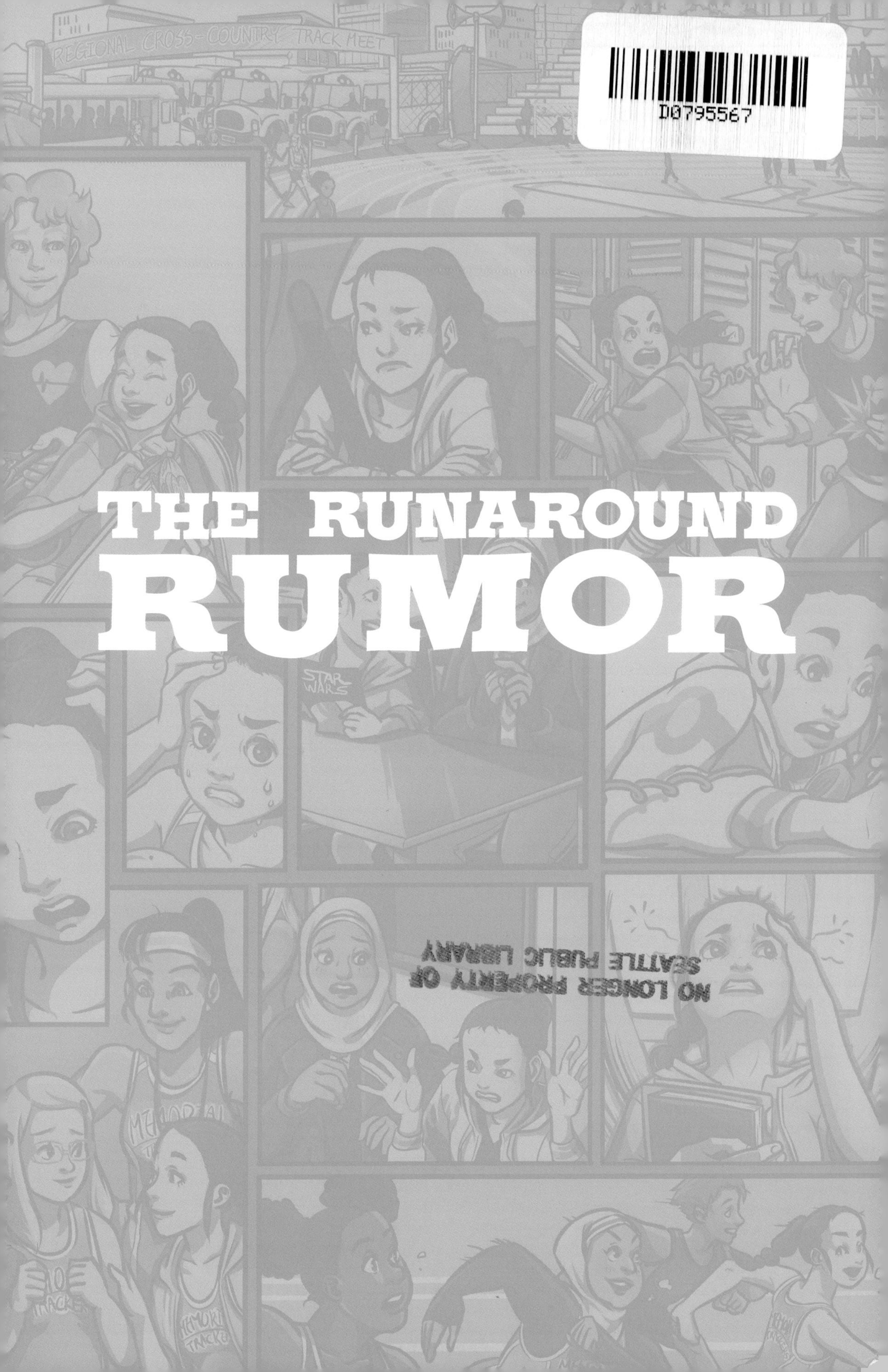
REGIONAL CROSS-COUNTRY TRACK MEET
Snatch!
STAR WARS

THE RUNAROUND RUMOR

JUNIOR HIGH DRAMA IS PUBLISHED BY
STONE ARCH BOOKS
A CAPSTONE IMPRINT
1710 ROE CREST DRIVE
NORTH MANKATO, MINNESOTA 56003
WWW.MYCAPSTONE.COM

Summary: Allie's world is turned upside down when she's diagnosed with diabetes. Her overprotective parents are driving her crazy, and she's desperate to keep her condition a secret from her friends. But her secretive ways are awfully suspicious and soon the rumors are flying. Is Allie's reputation ruined for good?

COPYRIGHT © 2019 STONE ARCH BOOKS
ALL RIGHTS RESERVED. NO PART OF THIS PUBLICATION MAY BE REPRODUCED IN WHOLE OR IN PART, OR STORED IN A RETRIEVAL SYSTEM, OR TRANSMITTED IN ANY FORM OR BY ANY MEANS, ELECTRONIC, MECHANICAL, PHOTOCOPYING, RECORDING, OR OTHERWISE, WITHOUT WRITTEN PERMISSION OF THE PUBLISHER.

CATALOGING-IN-PUBLICATION DATA IS AVAILABLE ON THE LIBRARY OF CONGRESS WEBSITE.
ISBN: 978-1-4965-4708-8 (LIBRARY BINDING)
ISBN: 978-1-4965-7413-8 (PAPERBACK)
ISBN: 978-1-4965-4713-2 (EBOOK PDF)

EDITOR: MARI BOLTE
DESIGNER: ASHLEE SUKER
CREATIVE DIRECTOR: NATHAN GASSMAN

Printed in the United States of America
PA017

JUNIOR HIGH DRAMA

THE RUNAROUND
RUMOR

by Louise Simonson   illustrated by Sumin Cho

STONE ARCH BOOKS
a capstone imprint

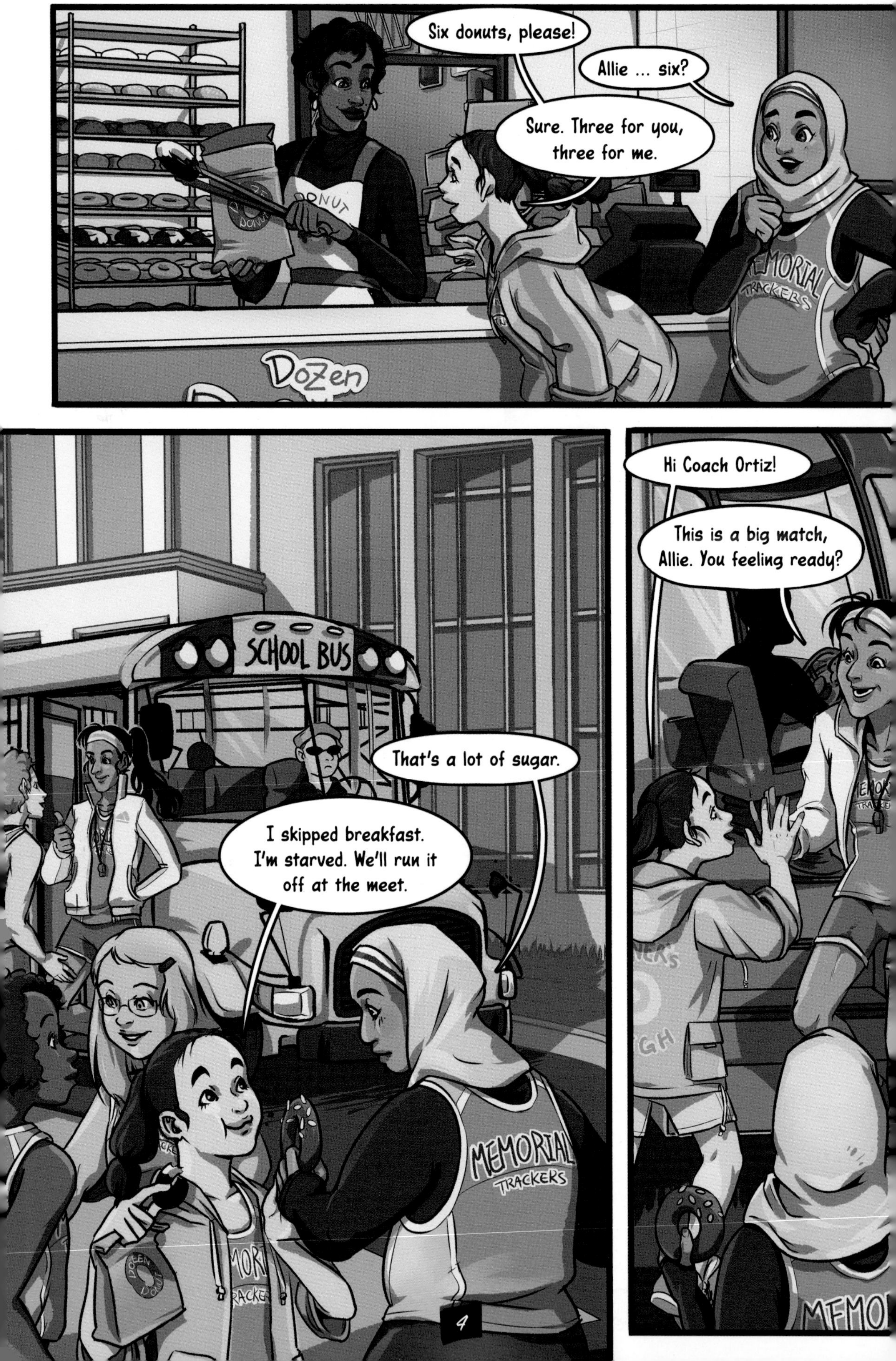
Six donuts, please!
Allie ... six?
Sure. Three for you, three for me.
DONUT
MEMORIAL TRACKERS
DoZen
SCHOOL BUS
That's a lot of sugar.
I skipped breakfast. I'm starved. We'll run it off at the meet.
MEMORIAL TRACKERS
Hi Coach Ortiz!
This is a big match, Allie. You feeling ready?

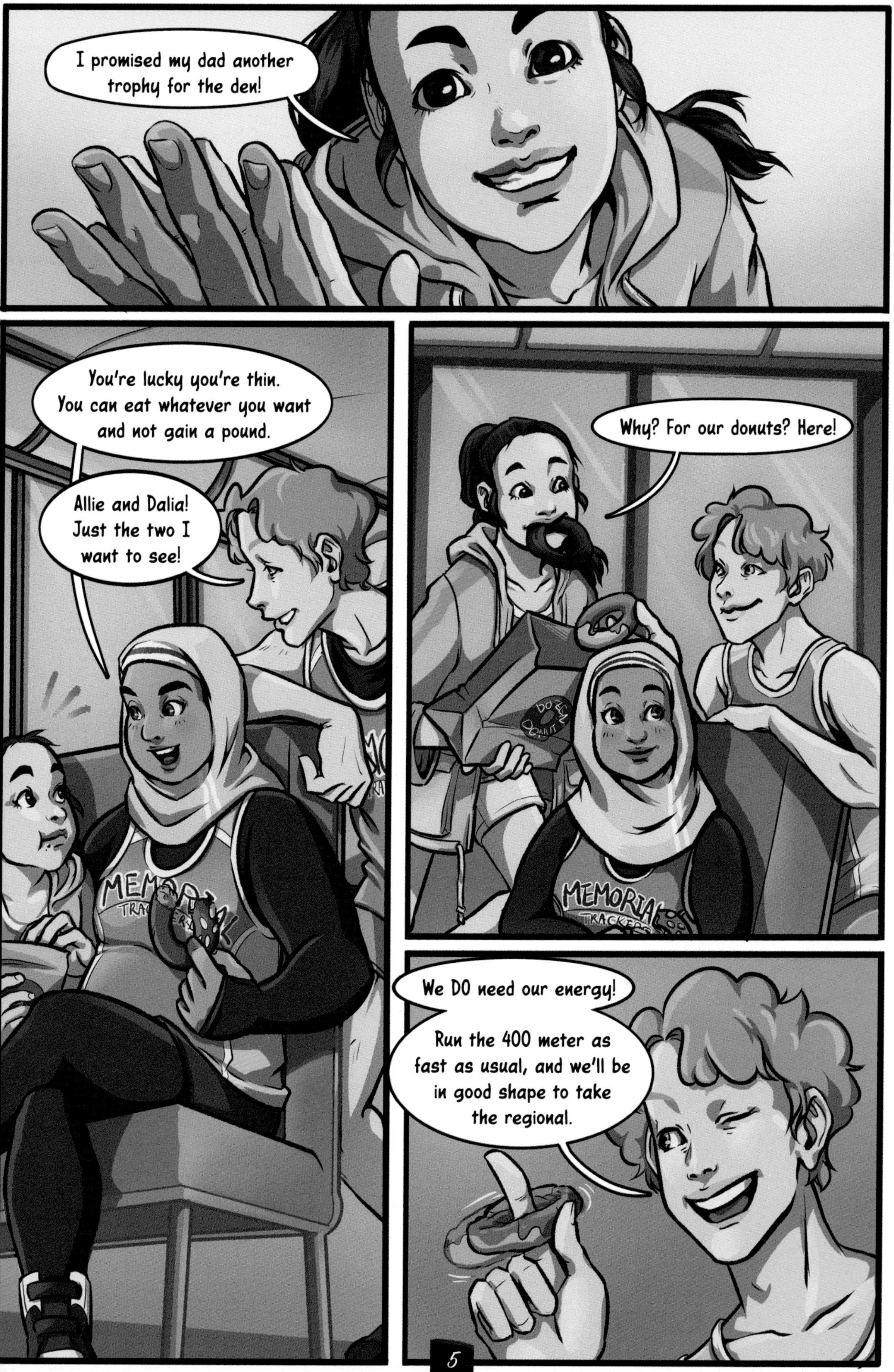
I promised my dad another trophy for the den!
You're lucky you're thin. You can eat whatever you want and not gain a pound.
Allie and Dalia! Just the two I want to see!
Why? For our donuts? Here!
We DO need our energy!
Run the 400 meter as fast as usual, and we'll be in good shape to take the regional.

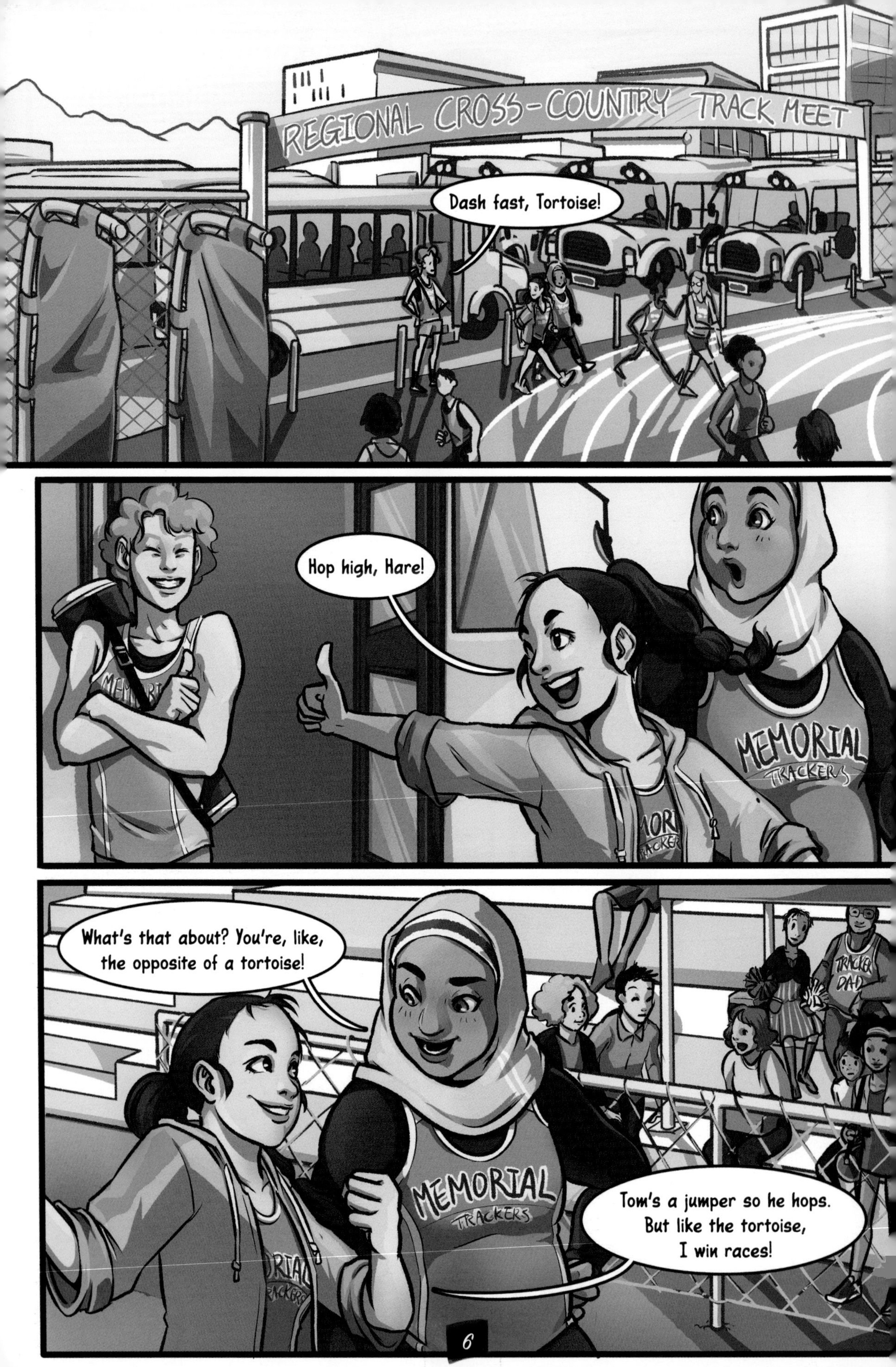
REGIONAL CROSS-COUNTRY TRACK MEET
Dash fast, Tortoise!
MEMORIAL
Hop high, Hare!
MEMORIAL TRACKERS
What's that about? You're, like, the opposite of a tortoise!
TRACKER DAD
MEMORIAL TRACKERS
Tom's a jumper so he hops. But like the tortoise, I win races!

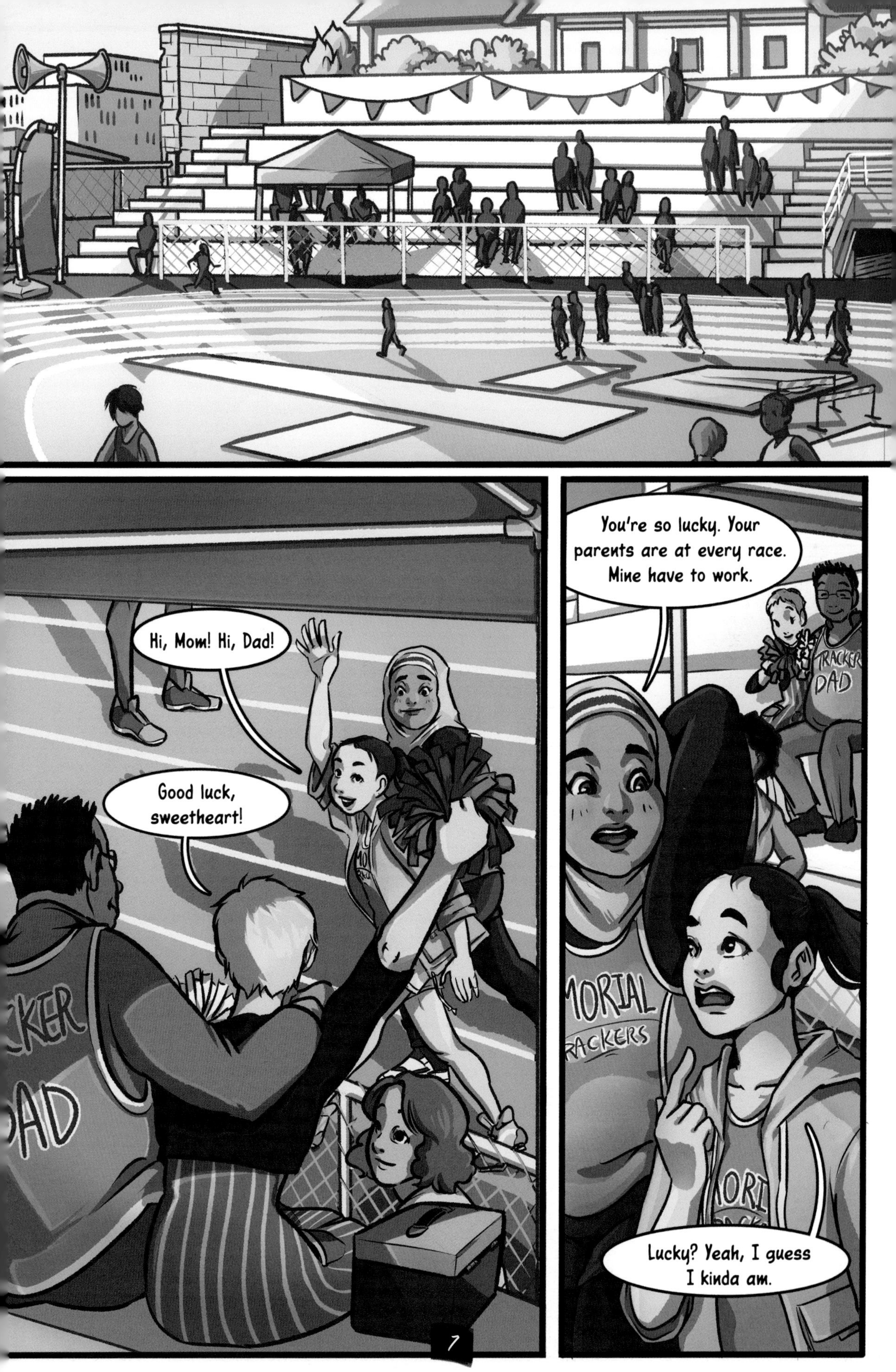
Hi, Mom! Hi, Dad!
Good luck, sweetheart!
TRACKER DAD
You're so lucky. Your parents are at every race. Mine have to work.
Lucky? Yeah, I guess I kinda am.

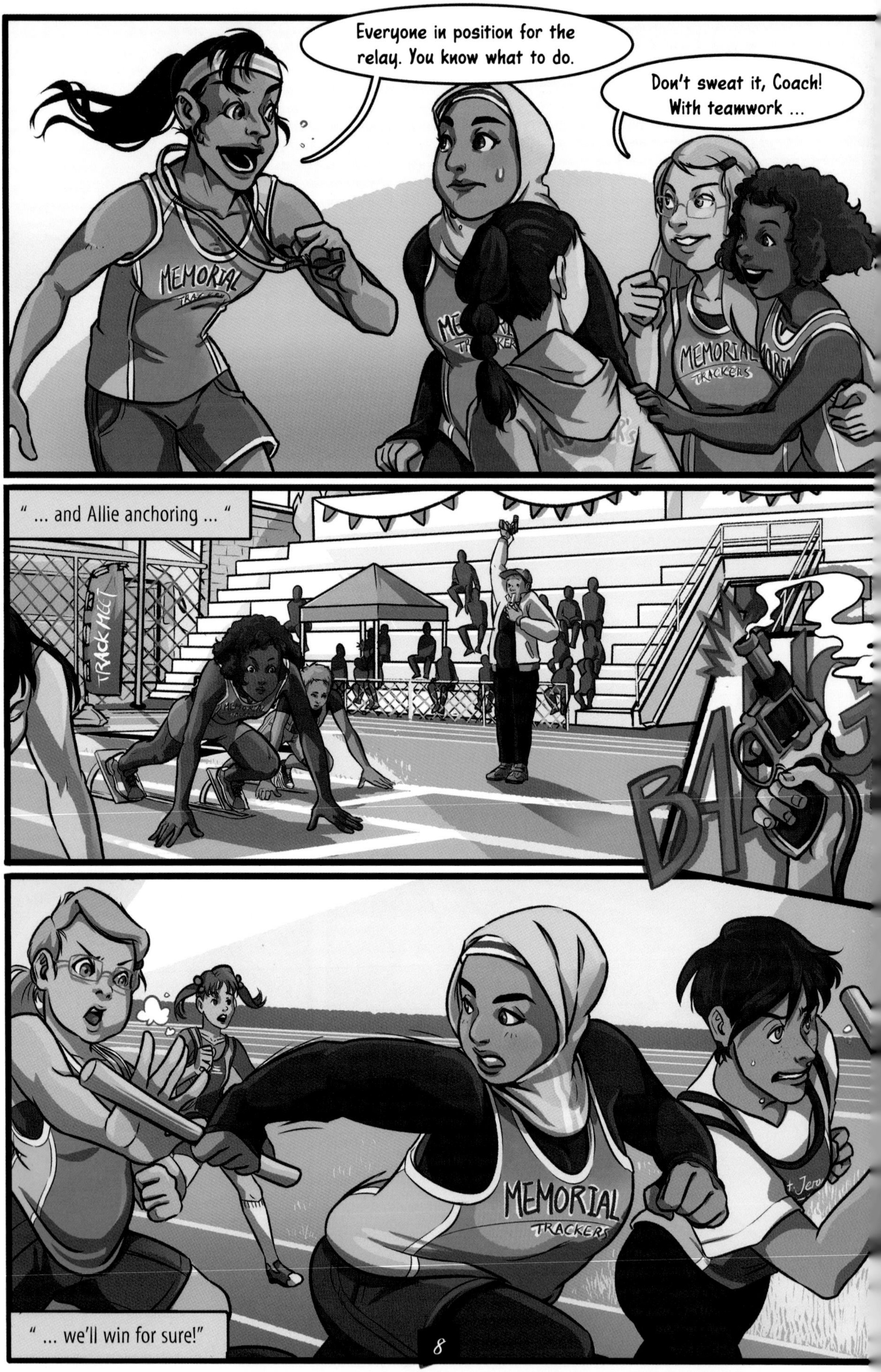
Everyone in position for the relay. You know what to do.
Don't sweat it, Coach! With teamwork ...
MEMORIAL TRACKERS
" ... and Allie anchoring ... "
TRACK MEET
BANG
MEMORIAL TRACKERS
" ... we'll win for sure!"

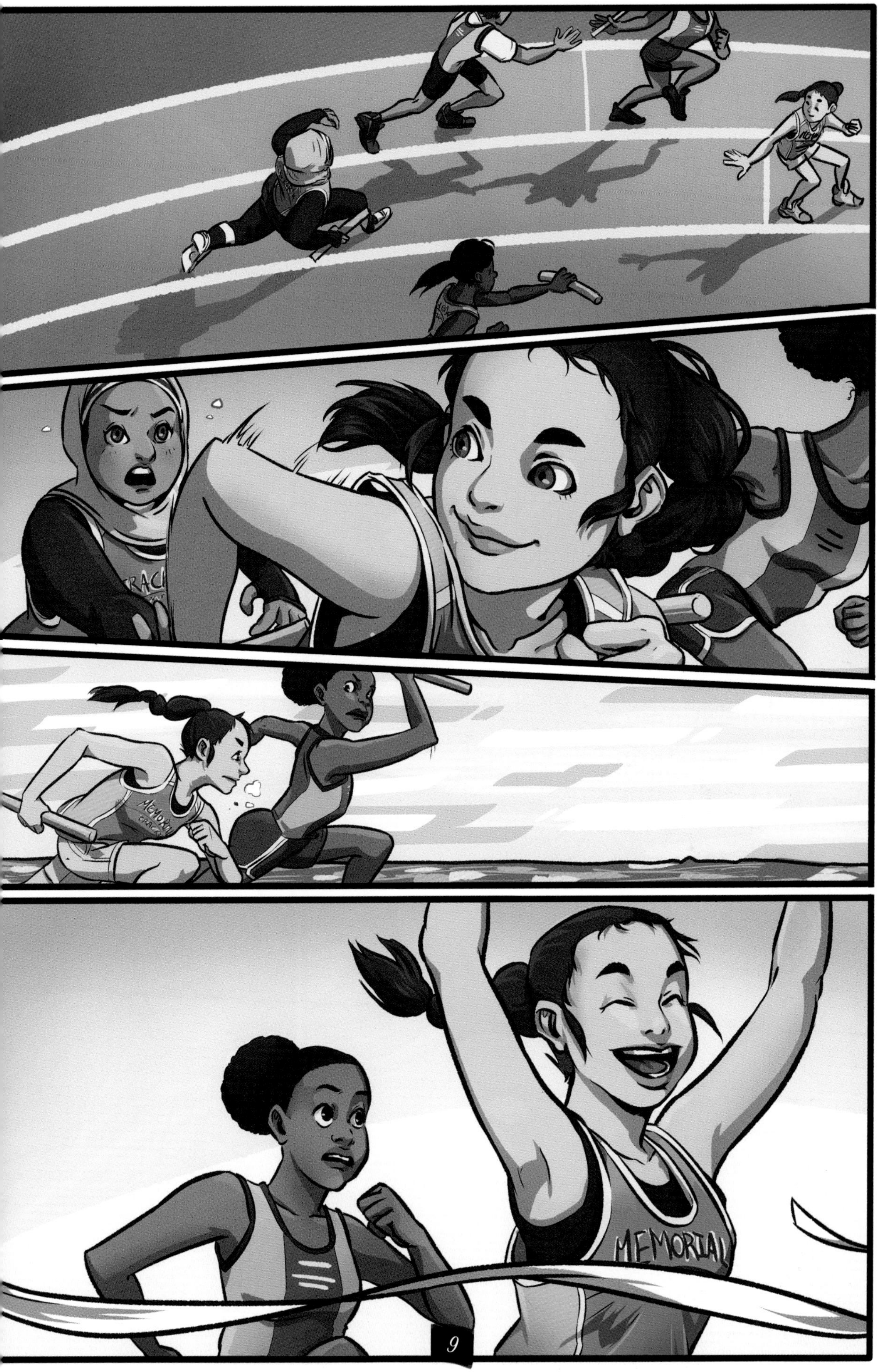
MEMORIAL

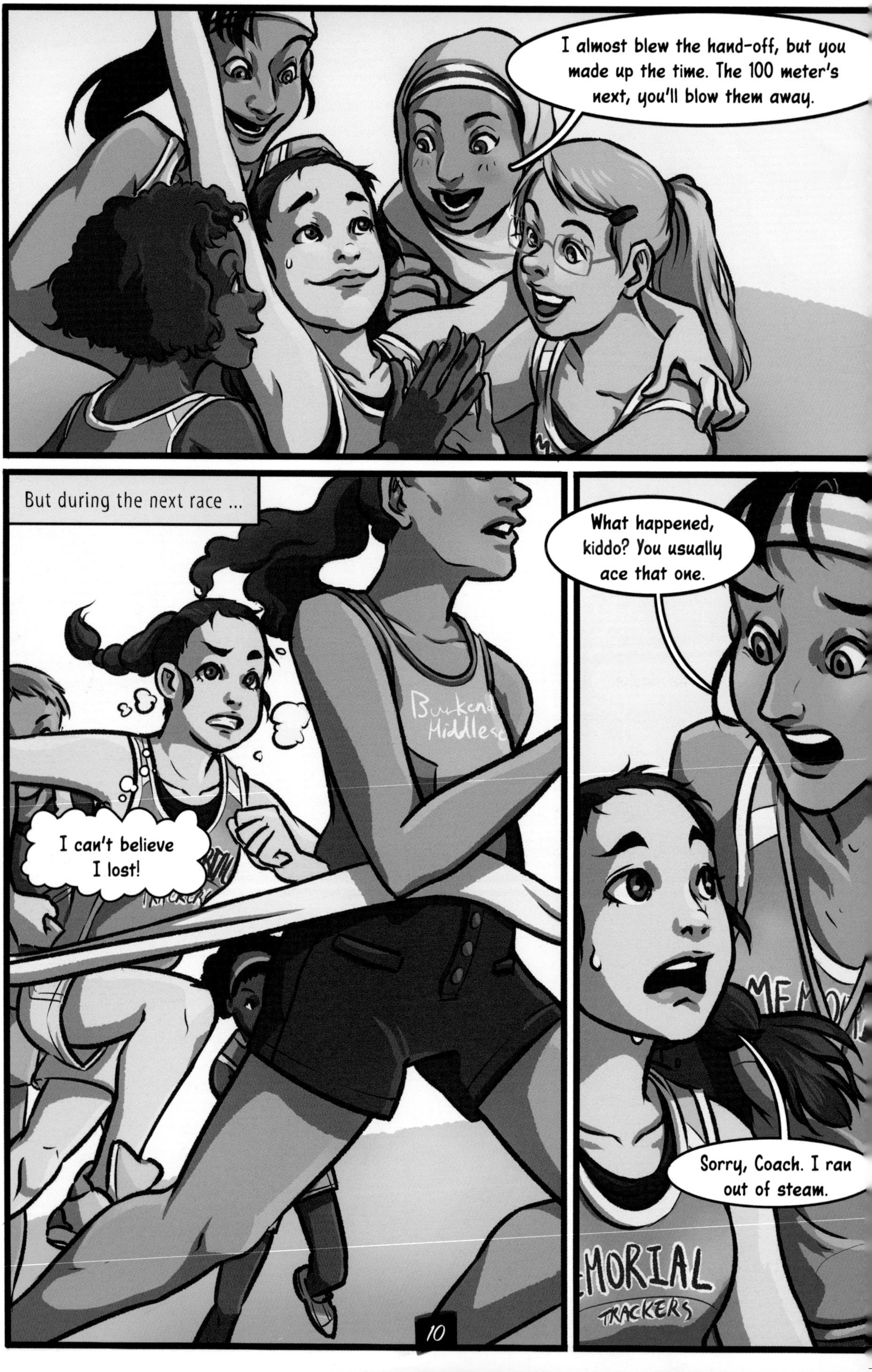
I almost blew the hand-off, but you made up the time. The 100 meter's next, you'll blow them away.
But during the next race ...
I can't believe I lost!
What happened, kiddo? You usually ace that one.
Sorry, Coach. I ran out of steam.

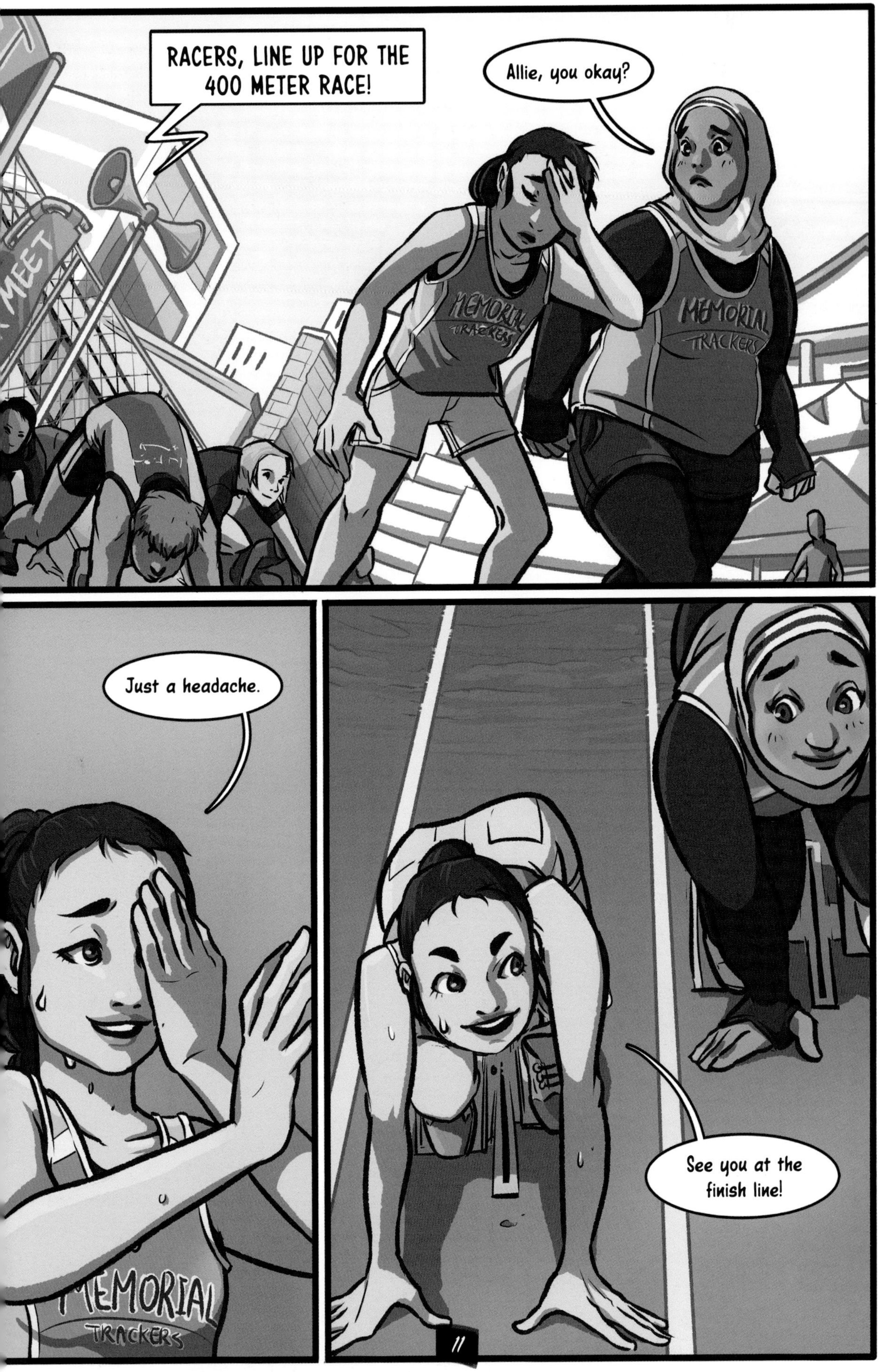
RACERS, LINE UP FOR THE 400 METER RACE!
Allie, you okay?
MEET
MEMORIAL TRACKERS
MEMORIAL TRACKERS
Just a headache.
MEMORIAL TRACKERS
See you at the finish line!
MEMORIAL TRACKERS

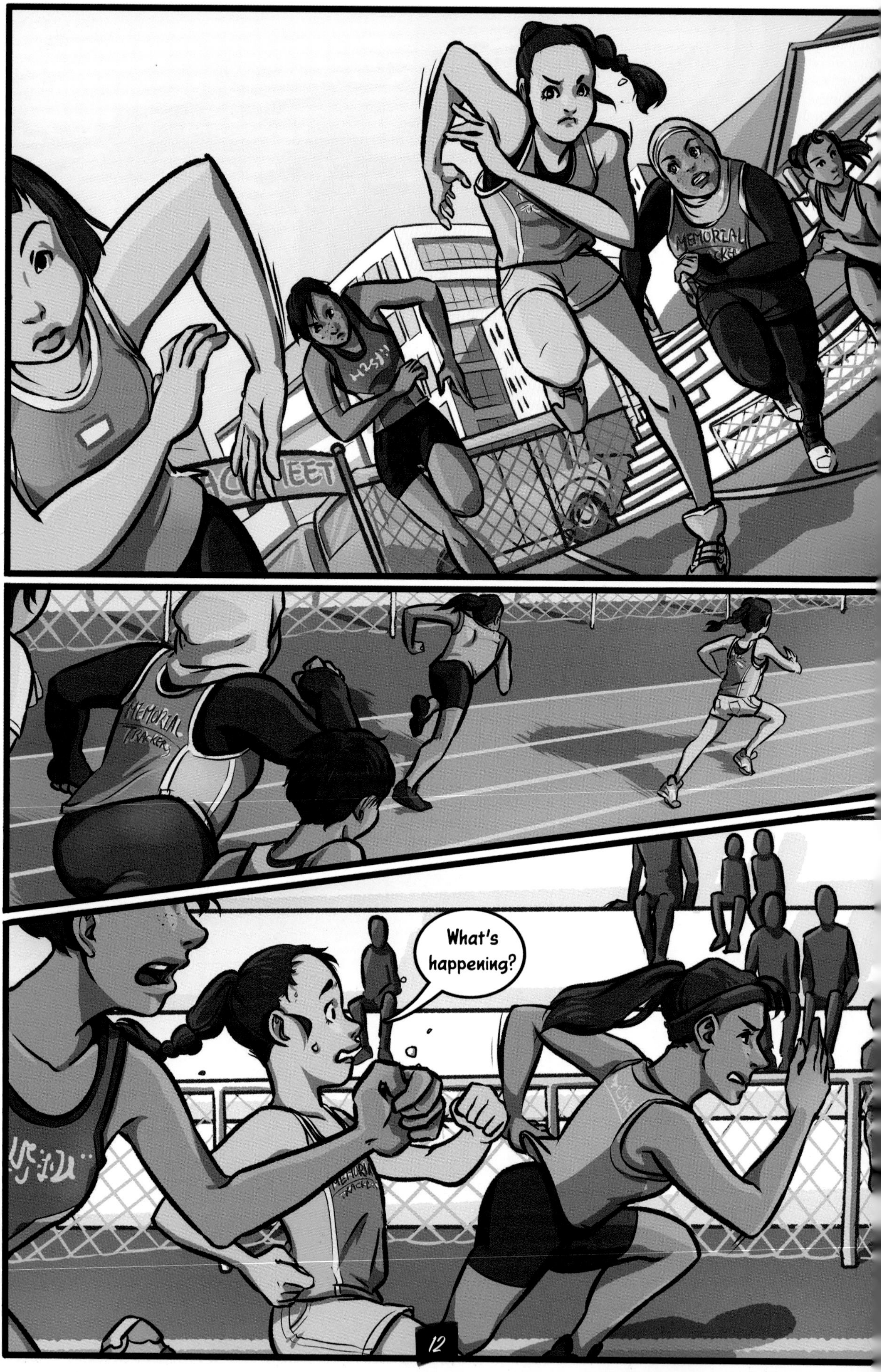
MEMORIAL TRACKERS
What's happening?

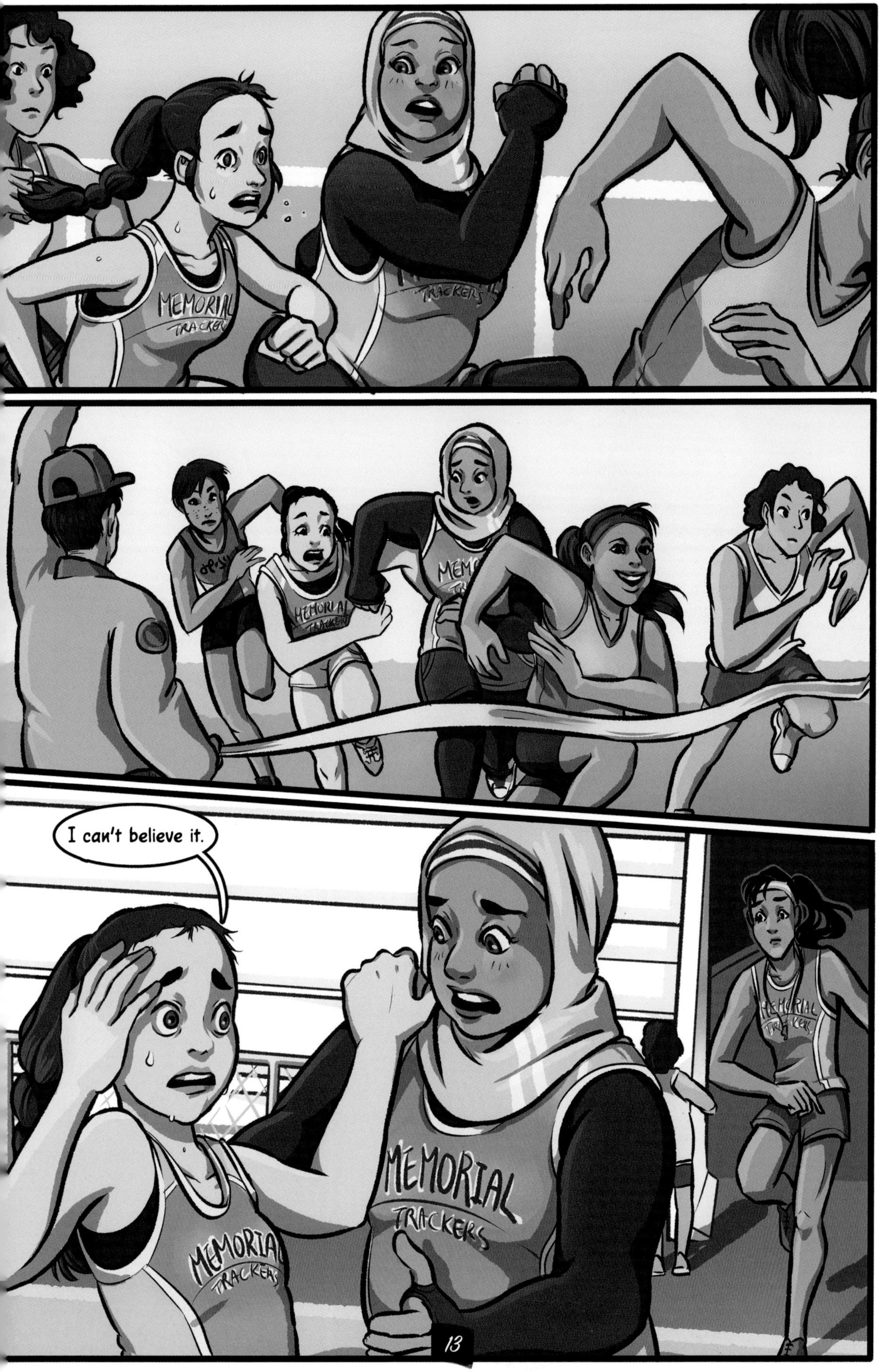
MEMORIAL
TRACKERS
TRACKERS
MEMORIAL
TRACKERS
MEMORIAL
I can't believe it.
MEMORIAL
TRACKERS
MEMORIAL
TRACKERS
MEMORIAL

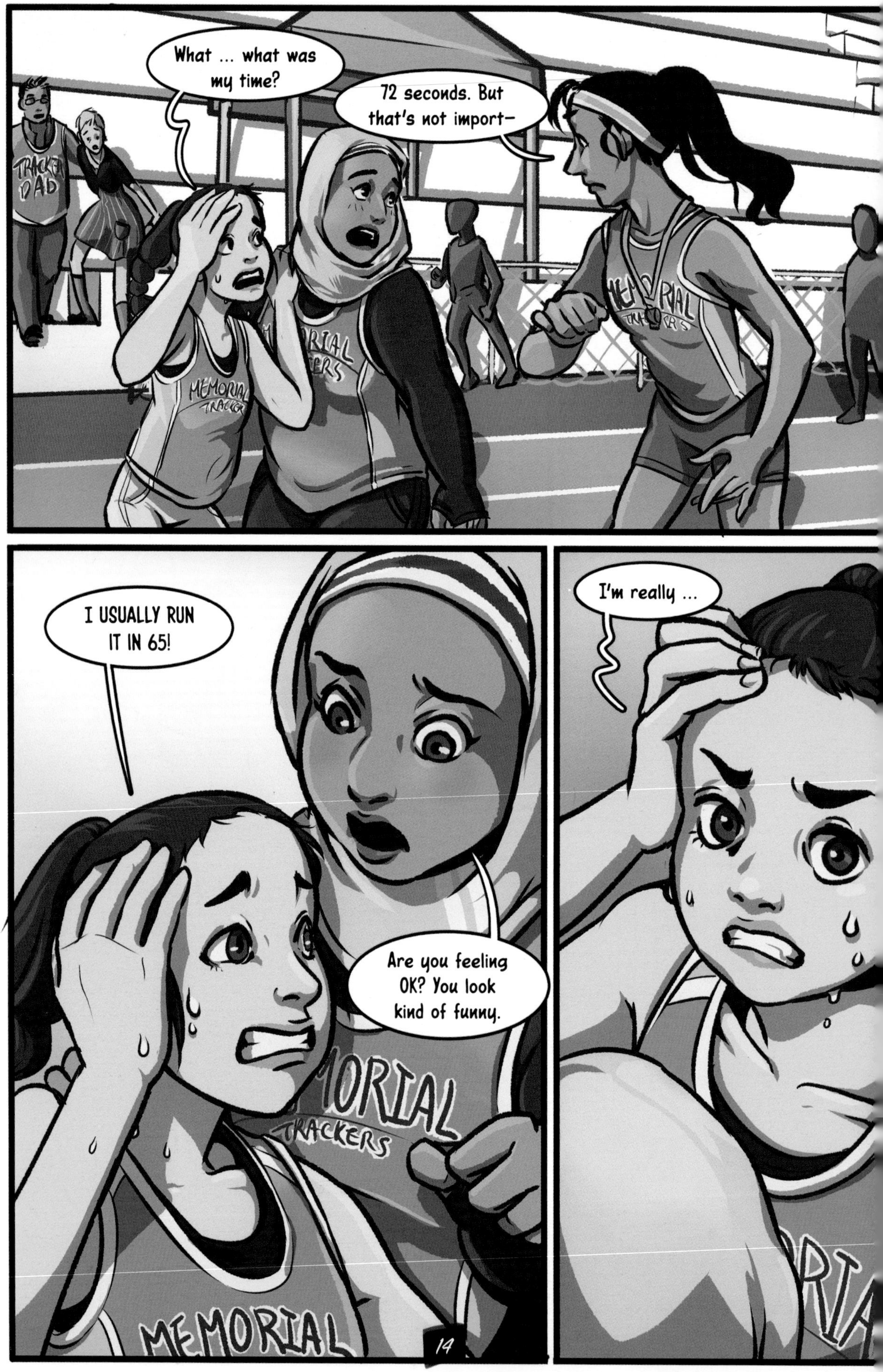

What ... what was my time?
72 seconds. But that's not import–
TRACKER DAD
MEMORIAL TRACKERS
I USUALLY RUN IT IN 65!
Are you feeling OK? You look kind of funny.
I'm really ...

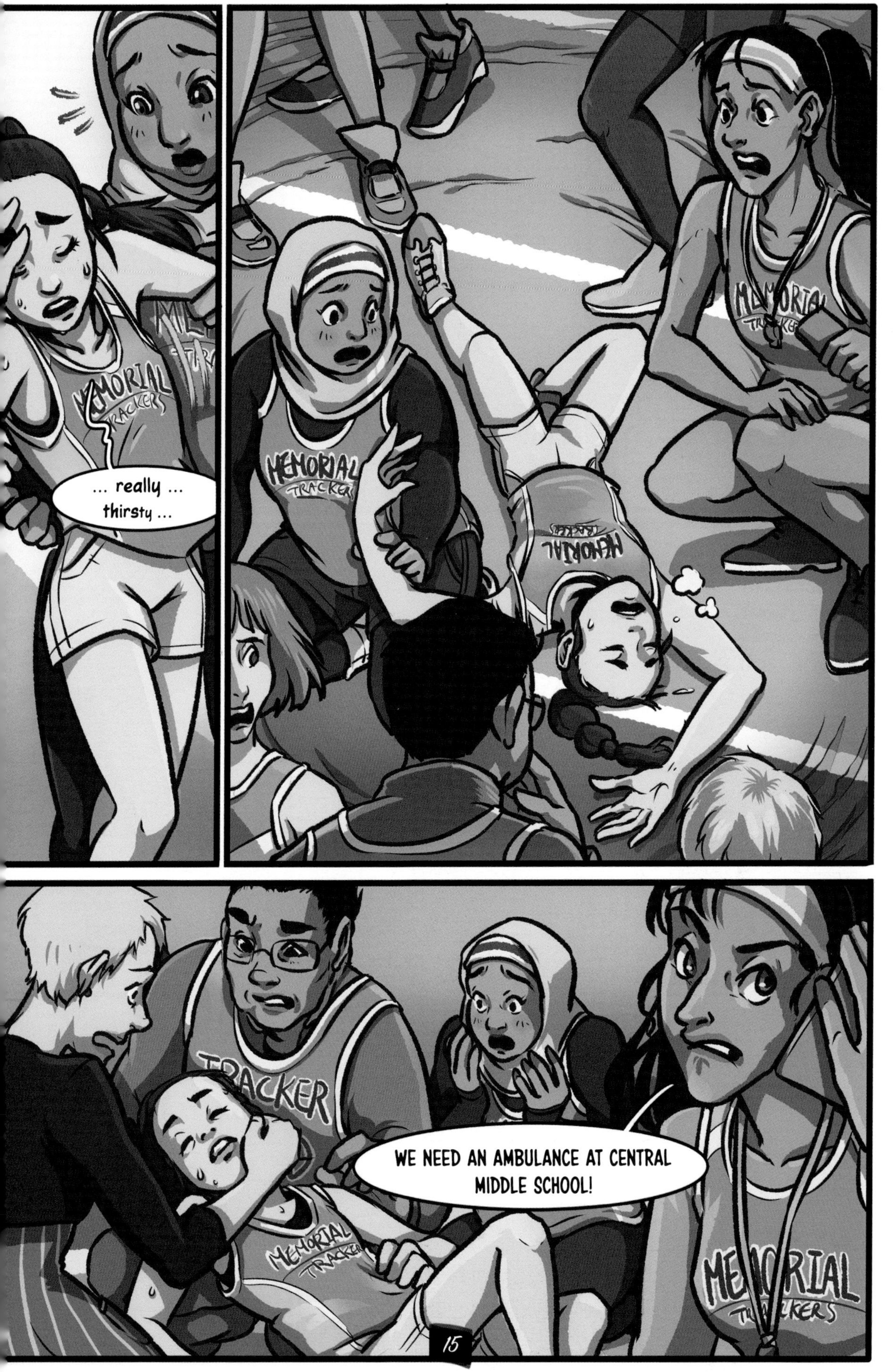

... really ... thirsty ...
WE NEED AN AMBULANCE AT CENTRAL MIDDLE SCHOOL!

A while later ...

Am I sick?

What happened?

Wh—what's wrong with me?

I lost ... !

Did Tom see me?

MEMORIAL TRACKERS

Patient drop off

Central EMERGENCY ROOM
+OPEN24

Hi, Allie. I'm Dr. Mansoor. Your parents tell me you had quite the fall.

We ran some tests while you were out.

It looks like you have type-1 diabetes.

What happened?

DIABETES?

What? Is it because she ate those donuts?

MEMORIAL TRACKERS

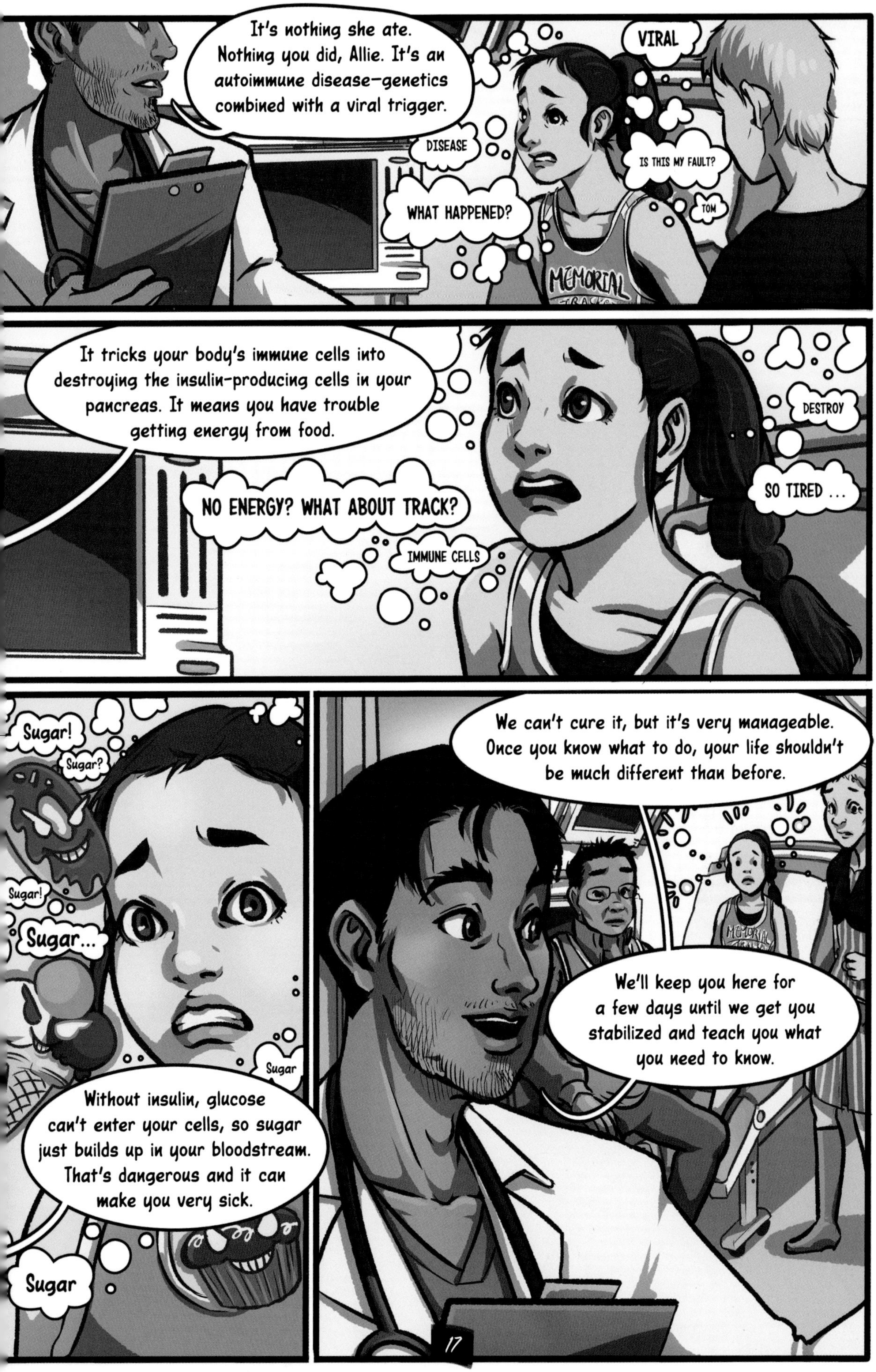
It's nothing she ate. Nothing you did, Allie. It's an autoimmune disease—genetics combined with a viral trigger.
VIRAL
DISEASE
IS THIS MY FAULT?
WHAT HAPPENED?
TOM
MEMORIAL
It tricks your body's immune cells into destroying the insulin-producing cells in your pancreas. It means you have trouble getting energy from food.
DESTROY
NO ENERGY? WHAT ABOUT TRACK?
SO TIRED . . .
IMMUNE CELLS
Sugar!
Sugar?
Sugar!
Sugar...
Sugar
Without insulin, glucose can't enter your cells, so sugar just builds up in your bloodstream. That's dangerous and it can make you very sick.
Sugar
We can't cure it, but it's very manageable. Once you know what to do, your life shouldn't be much different than before.
MEMORIAL
We'll keep you here for a few days until we get you stabilized and teach you what you need to know.

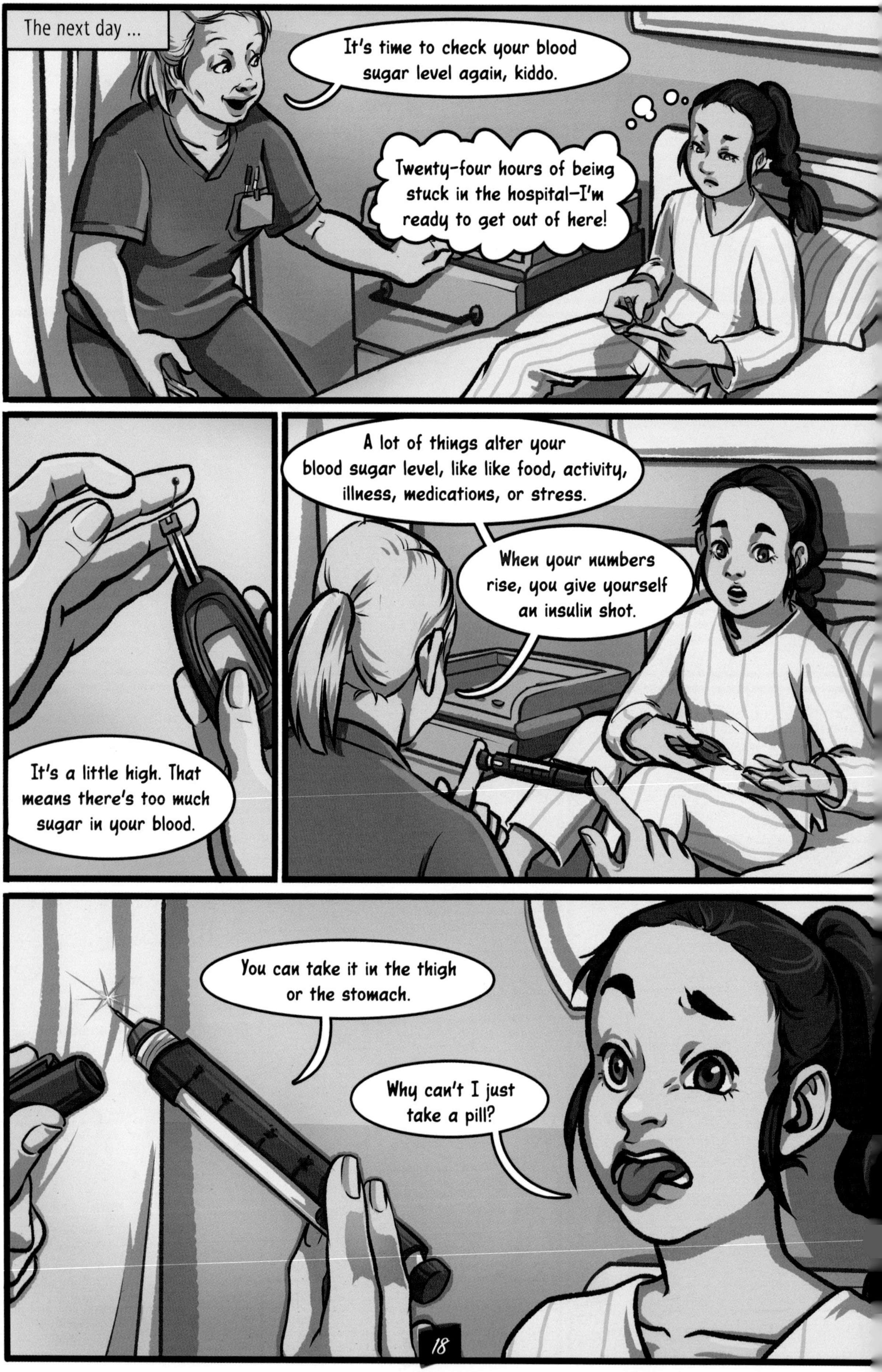
The next day ...
It's time to check your blood sugar level again, kiddo.
Twenty-four hours of being stuck in the hospital—I'm ready to get out of here!
It's a little high. That means there's too much sugar in your blood.
A lot of things alter your blood sugar level, like like food, activity, illness, medications, or stress.
When your numbers rise, you give yourself an insulin shot.
You can take it in the thigh or the stomach.
Why can't I just take a pill?

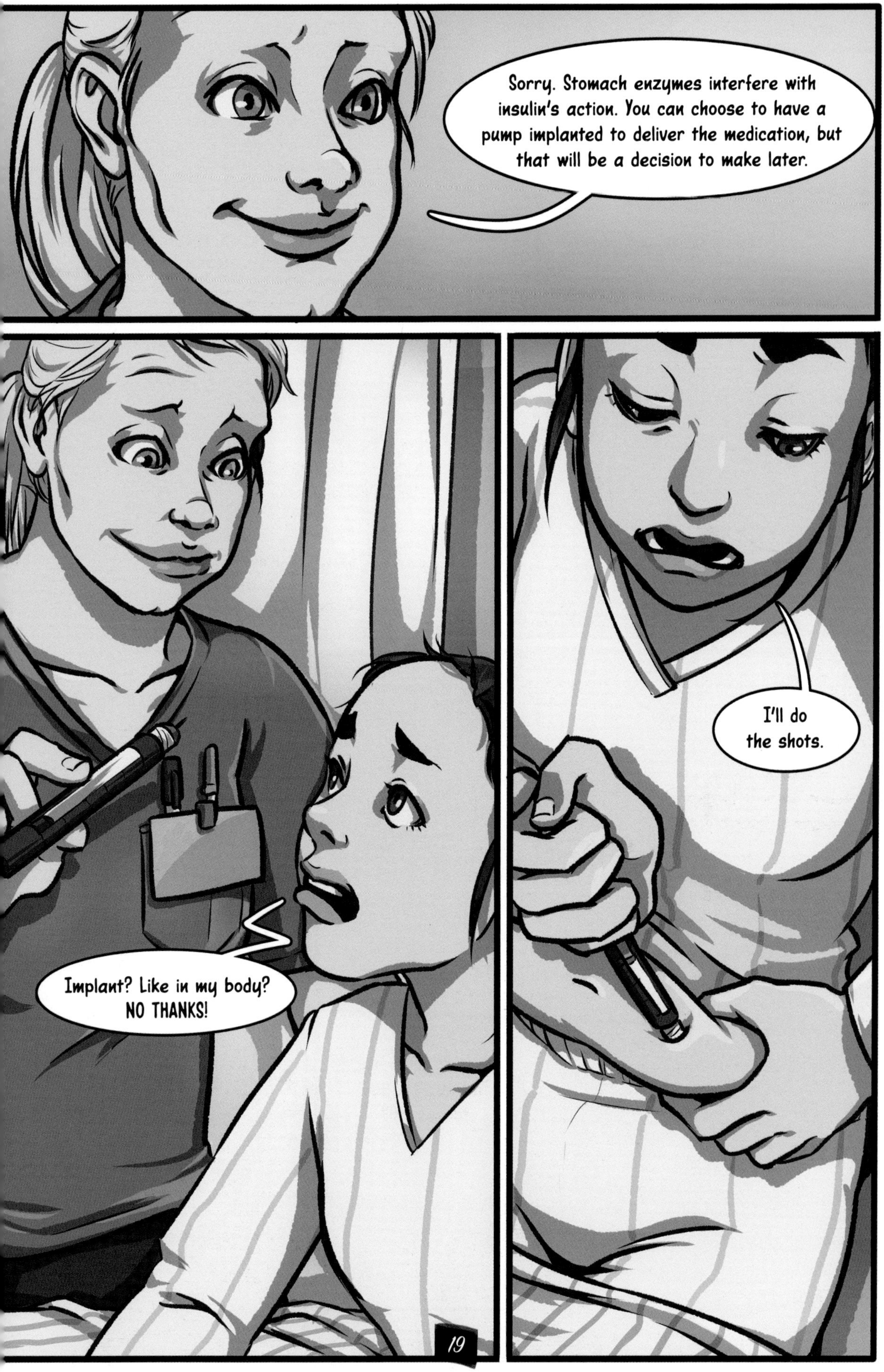
Sorry. Stomach enzymes interfere with insulin's action. You can choose to have a pump implanted to deliver the medication, but that will be a decision to make later.
Implant? Like in my body? NO THANKS!
I'll do the shots.

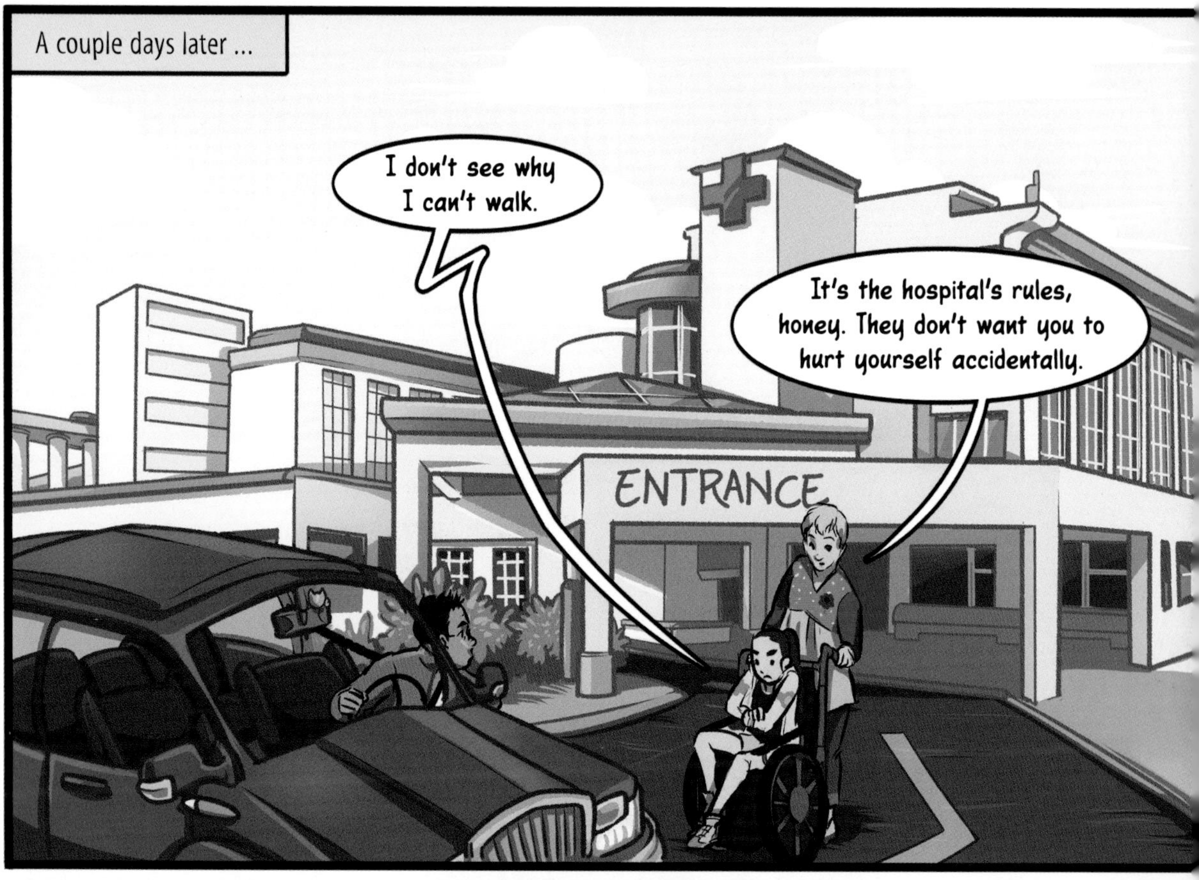
A couple days later ...
I don't see why I can't walk.
It's the hospital's rules, honey. They don't want you to hurt yourself accidentally.
ENTRANCE

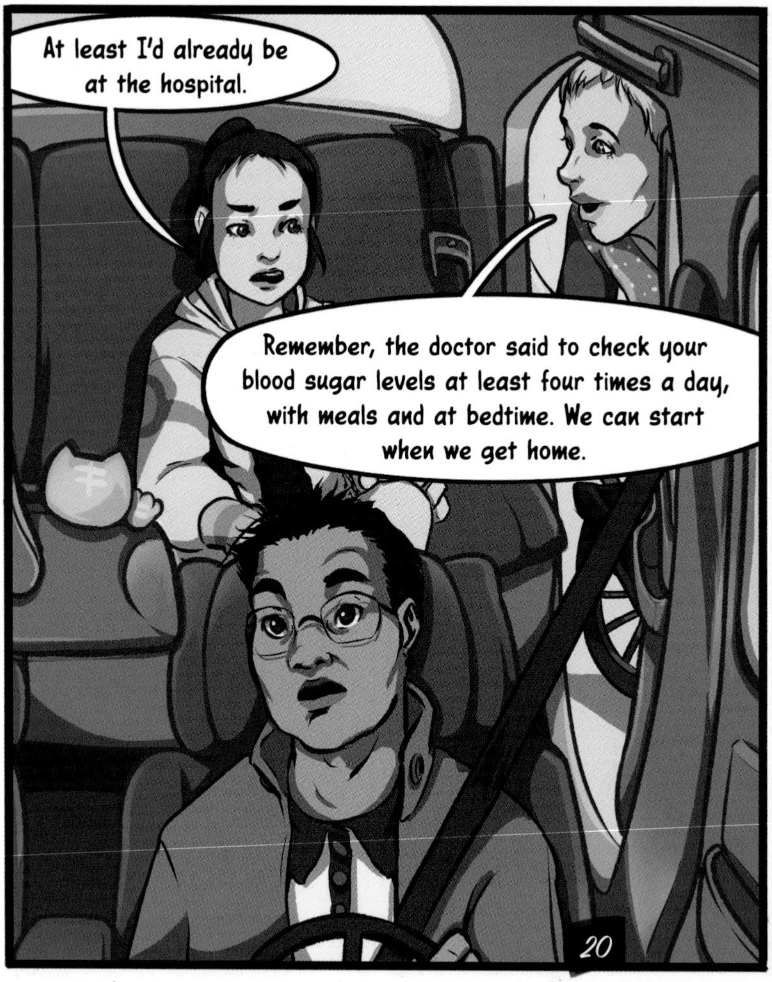
At least I'd already be at the hospital.
Remember, the doctor said to check your blood sugar levels at least four times a day, with meals and at bedtime. We can start when we get home.

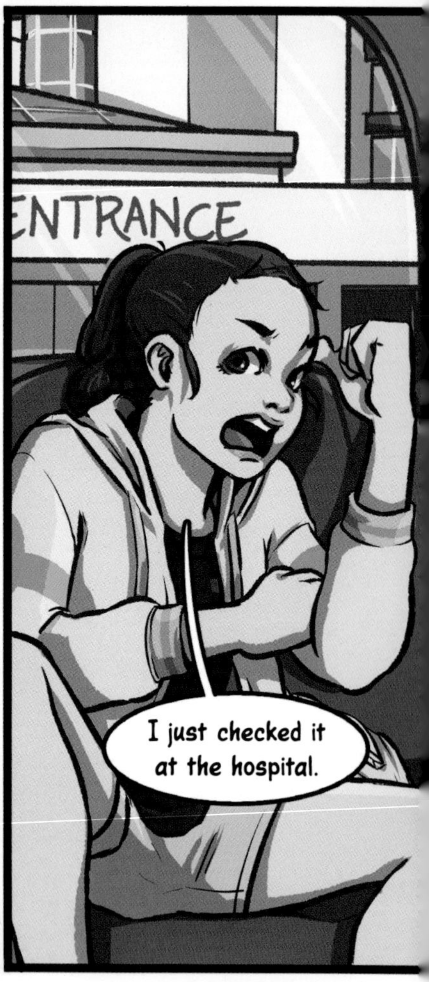
ENTRANCE
I just checked it at the hospital.

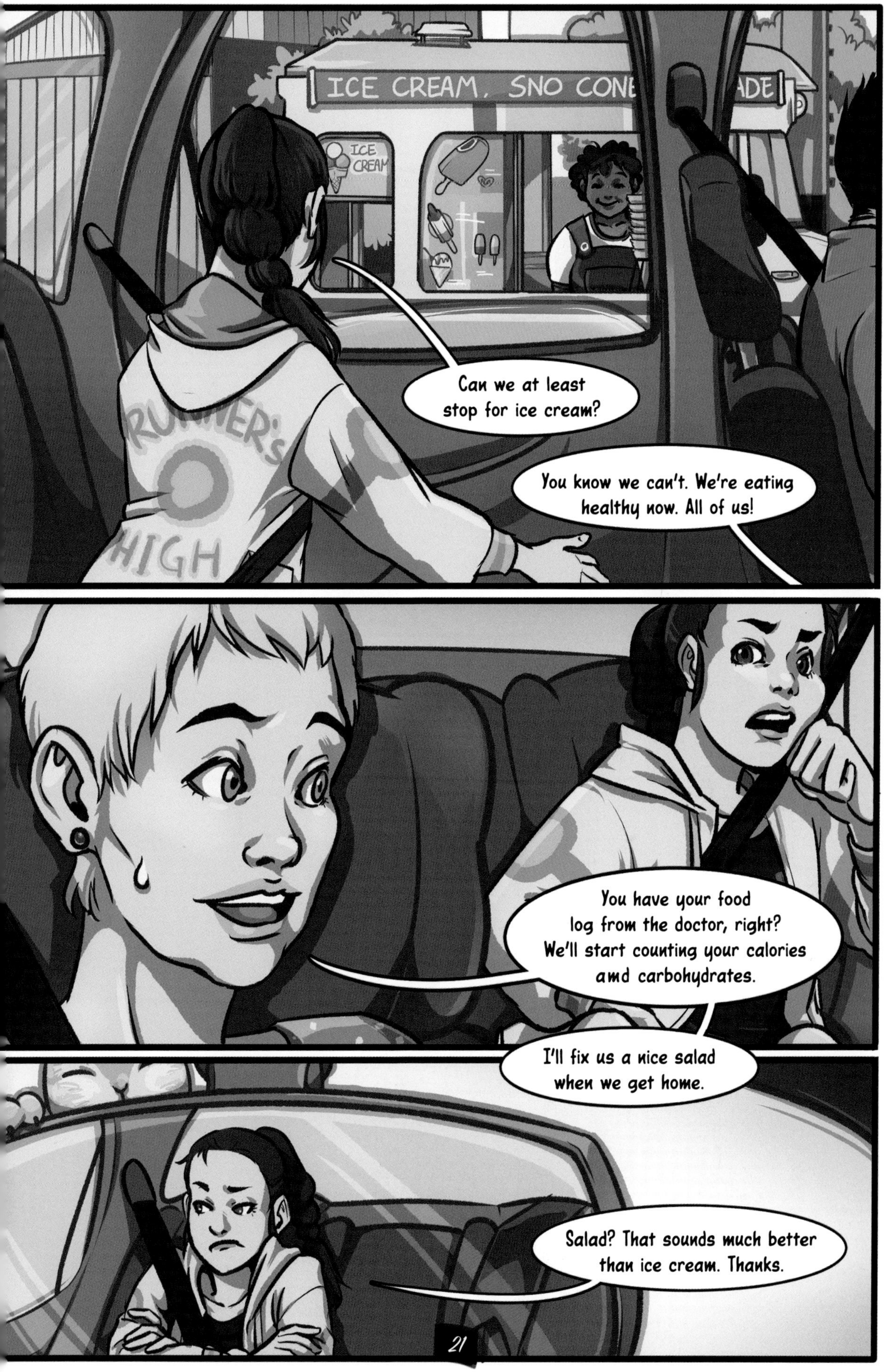
ICE CREAM, SNO CONE ADE
ICE CREAM
RUNNER'S HIGH
Can we at least stop for ice cream?
You know we can't. We're eating healthy now. All of us!
You have your food log from the doctor, right? We'll start counting your calories amd carbohydrates.
I'll fix us a nice salad when we get home.
Salad? That sounds much better than ice cream. Thanks.

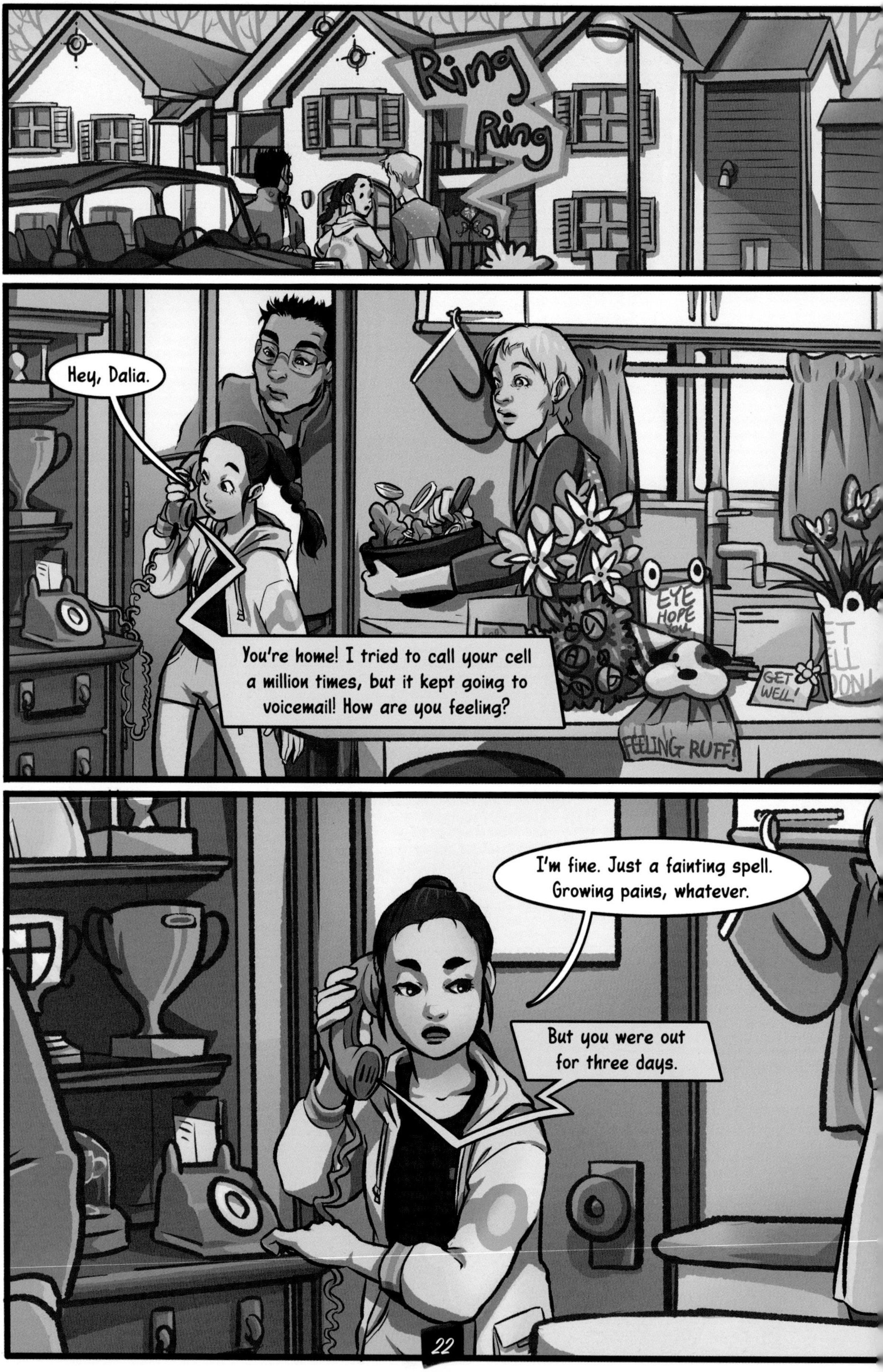
Ring Ring
Hey, Dalia.
You're home! I tried to call your cell a million times, but it kept going to voicemail! How are you feeling?
EYE HOPE YOU
GET WELL!
FEELING RUFF?
I'm fine. Just a fainting spell. Growing pains, whatever.
But you were out for three days.

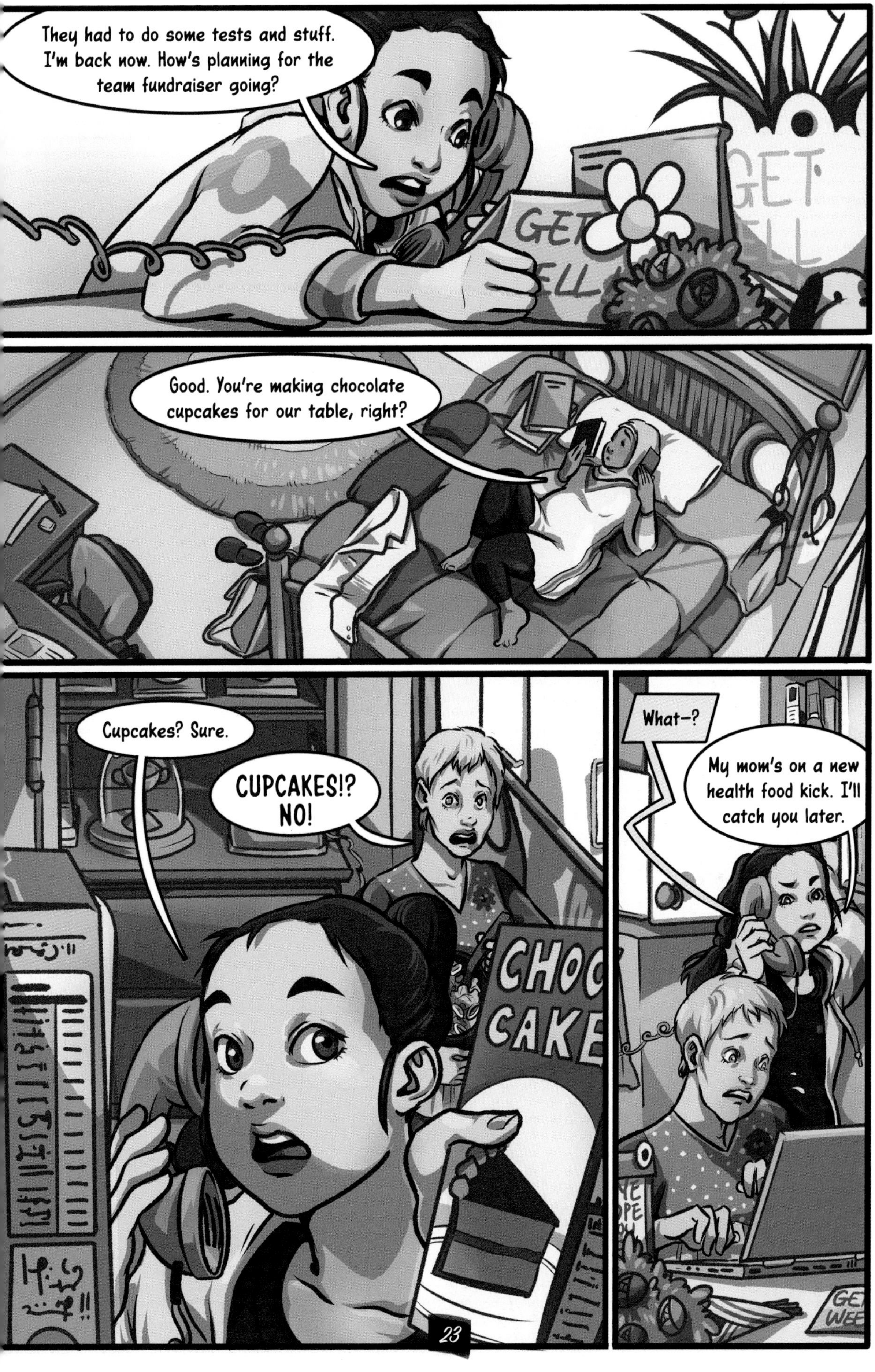
They had to do some tests and stuff. I'm back now. How's planning for the team fundraiser going?
GET WELL
GET WELL
Good. You're making chocolate cupcakes for our table, right?
Cupcakes? Sure.
CUPCAKES!? NO!
CHOC CAKE
What–?
My mom's on a new health food kick. I'll catch you later.

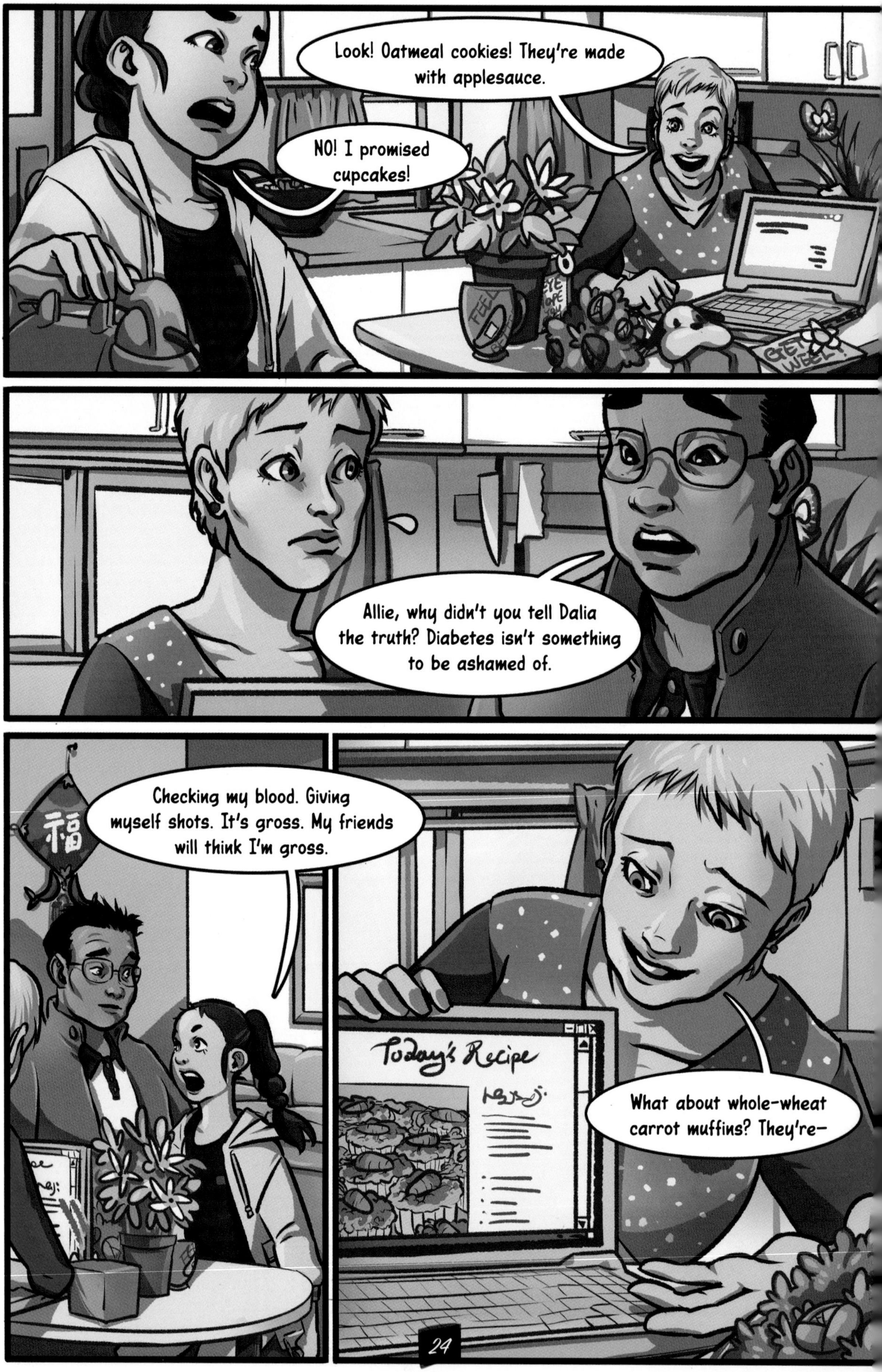
Look! Oatmeal cookies! They're made with applesauce.
NO! I promised cupcakes!
GET WELL
Allie, why didn't you tell Dalia the truth? Diabetes isn't something to be ashamed of.
Checking my blood. Giving myself shots. It's gross. My friends will think I'm gross.
Today's Recipe
What about whole-wheat carrot muffins? They're–

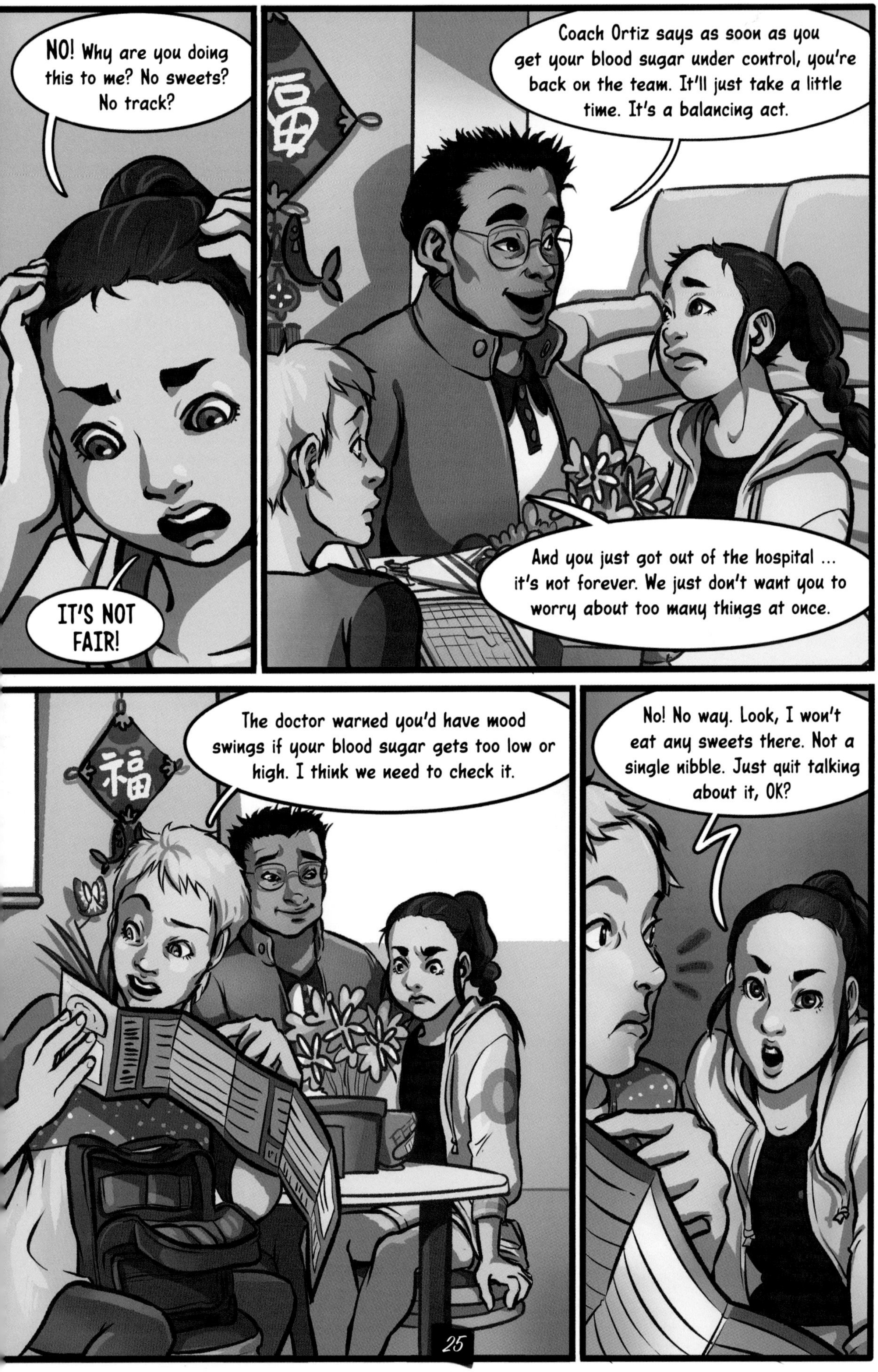
NO! Why are you doing this to me? No sweets? No track?
IT'S NOT FAIR!
Coach Ortiz says as soon as you get your blood sugar under control, you're back on the team. It'll just take a little time. It's a balancing act.
And you just got out of the hospital ... it's not forever. We just don't want you to worry about too many things at once.
The doctor warned you'd have mood swings if your blood sugar gets too low or high. I think we need to check it.
No! No way. Look, I won't eat any sweets there. Not a single nibble. Just quit talking about it, OK?

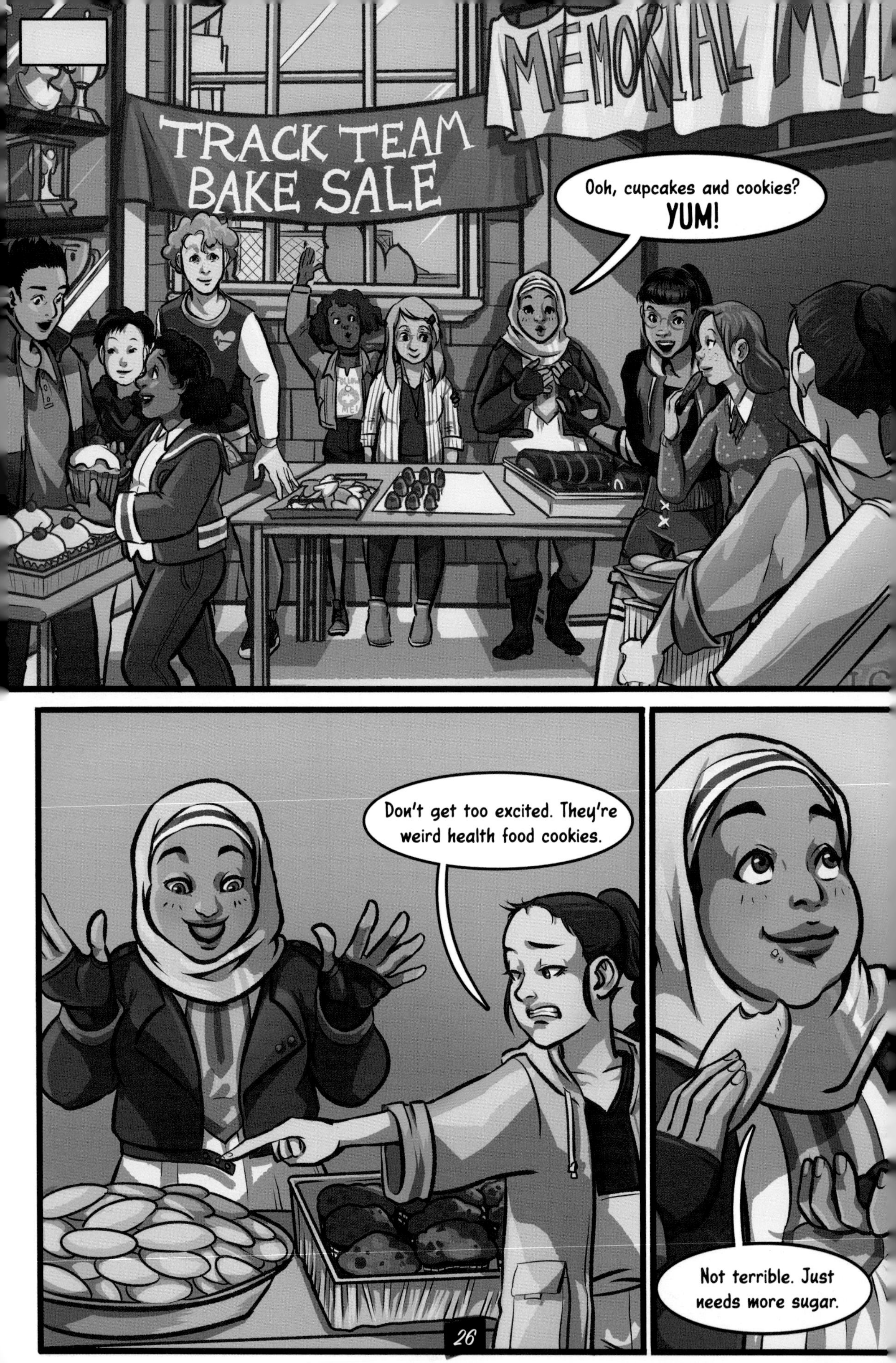
TRACK TEAM BAKE SALE
MEMORIAL
Ooh, cupcakes and cookies? YUM!
Don't get too excited. They're weird health food cookies.
Not terrible. Just needs more sugar.

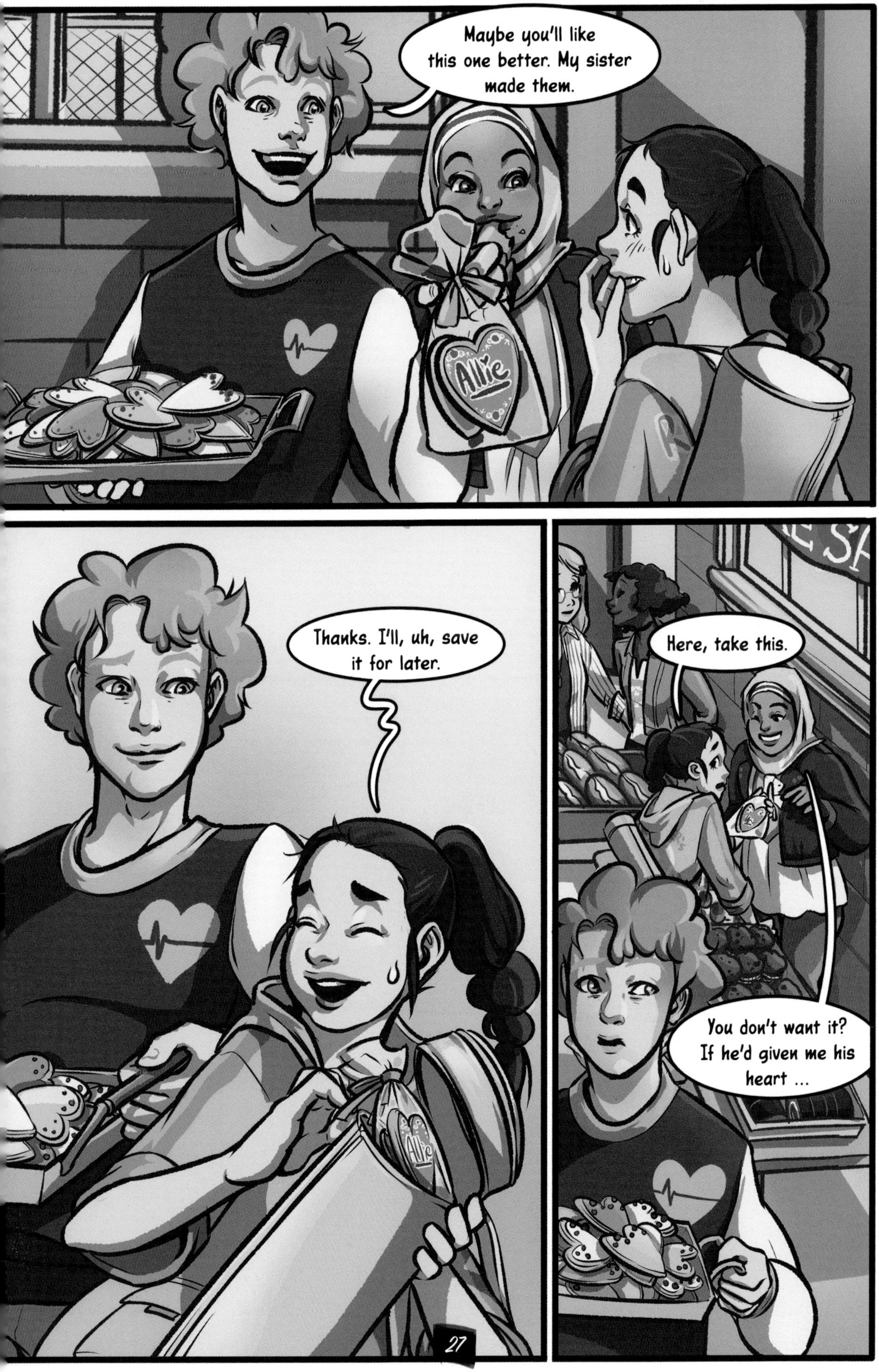

Maybe you'll like this one better. My sister made them.
Allie
Thanks. I'll, uh, save it for later.
Allie
Here, take this.
You don't want it? If he'd given me his heart ...

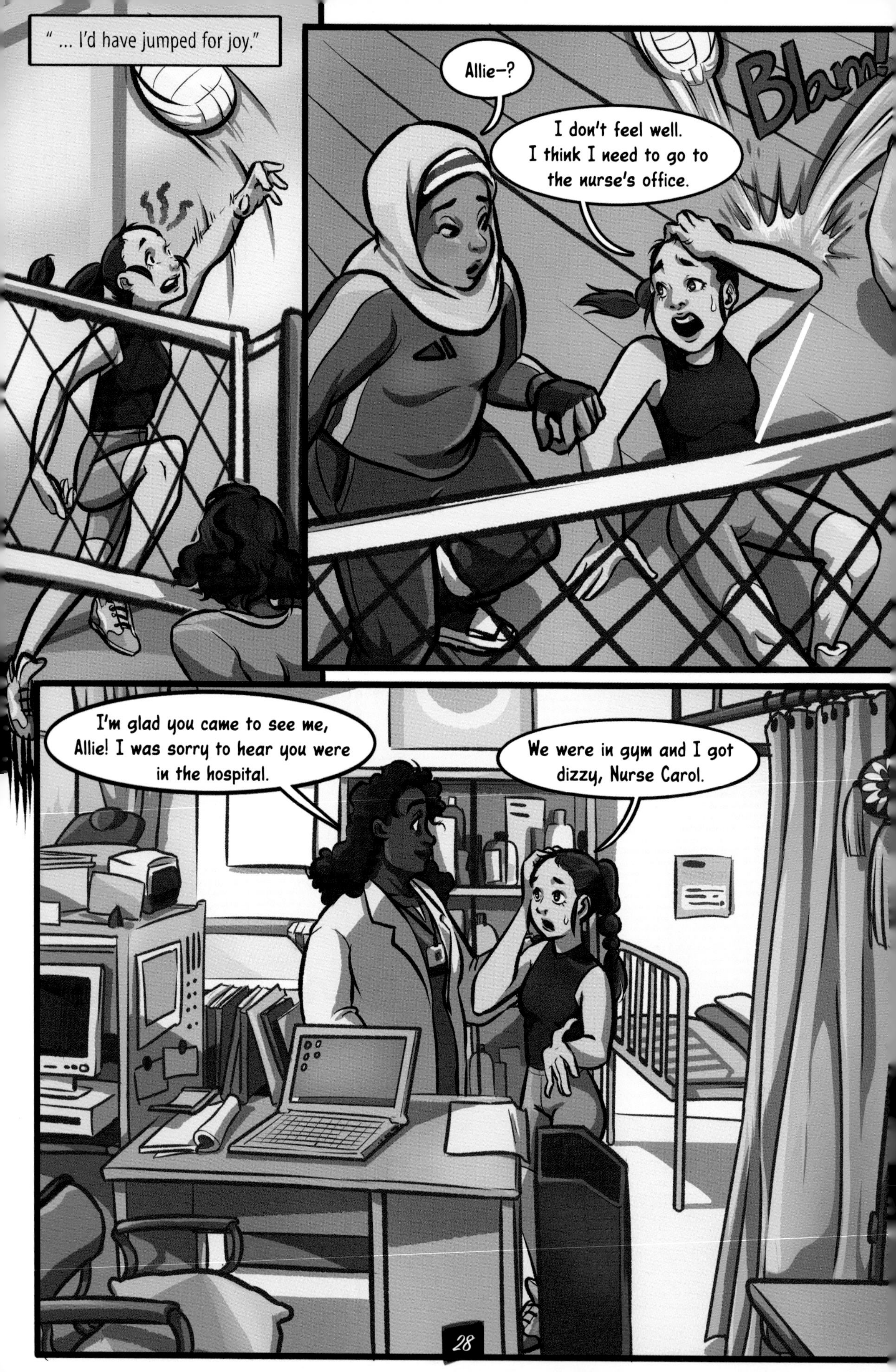
" ... I'd have jumped for joy."
Allie–?
Blam!
I don't feel well. I think I need to go to the nurse's office.
I'm glad you came to see me, Allie! I was sorry to hear you were in the hospital.
We were in gym and I got dizzy, Nurse Carol.

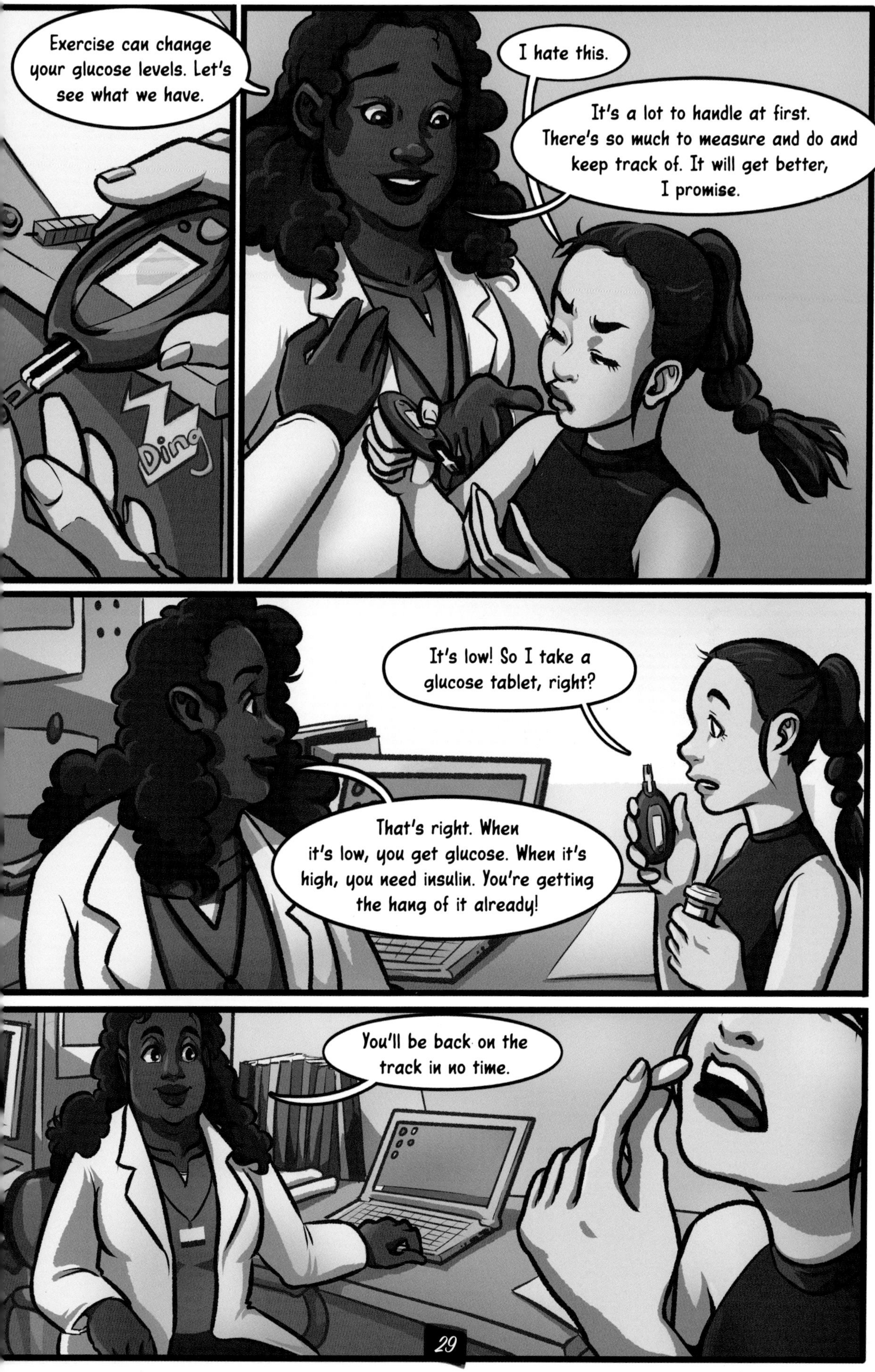
Exercise can change your glucose levels. Let's see what we have.
Ding
I hate this.
It's a lot to handle at first. There's so much to measure and do and keep track of. It will get better, I promise.
It's low! So I take a glucose tablet, right?
That's right. When it's low, you get glucose. When it's high, you need insulin. You're getting the hang of it already!
You'll be back on the track in no time.

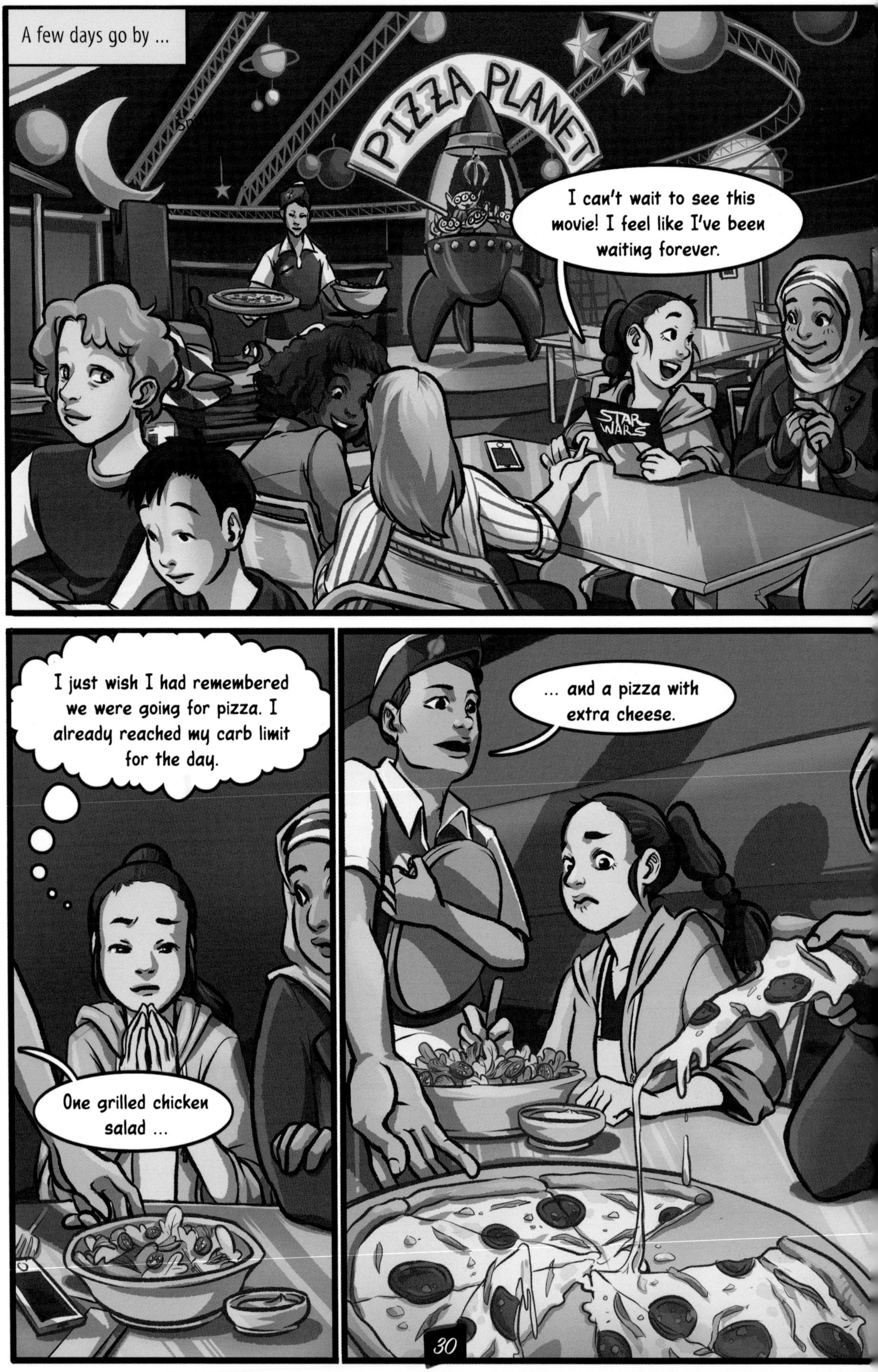
A few days go by ...
PIZZA PLANET
I can't wait to see this movie! I feel like I've been waiting forever.
STAR WARS
I just wish I had remembered we were going for pizza. I already reached my carb limit for the day.
One grilled chicken salad ...
... and a pizza with extra cheese.

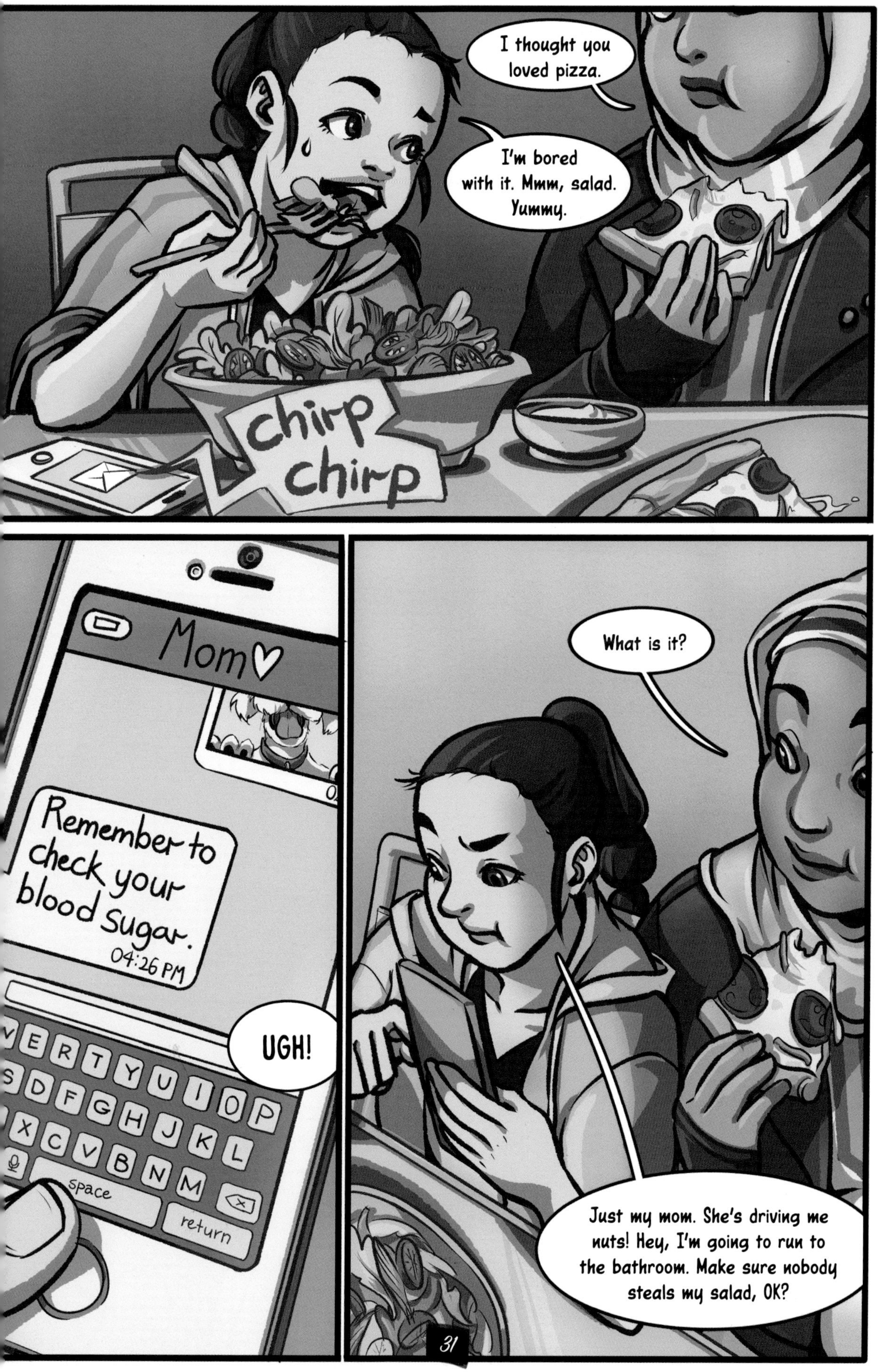
I thought you loved pizza.
I'm bored with it. Mmm, salad. Yummy.
chirp chirp
Mom
Remember to check your blood sugar.
04:26 PM
UGH!
What is it?
Just my mom. She's driving me nuts! Hey, I'm going to run to the bathroom. Make sure nobody steals my salad, OK?

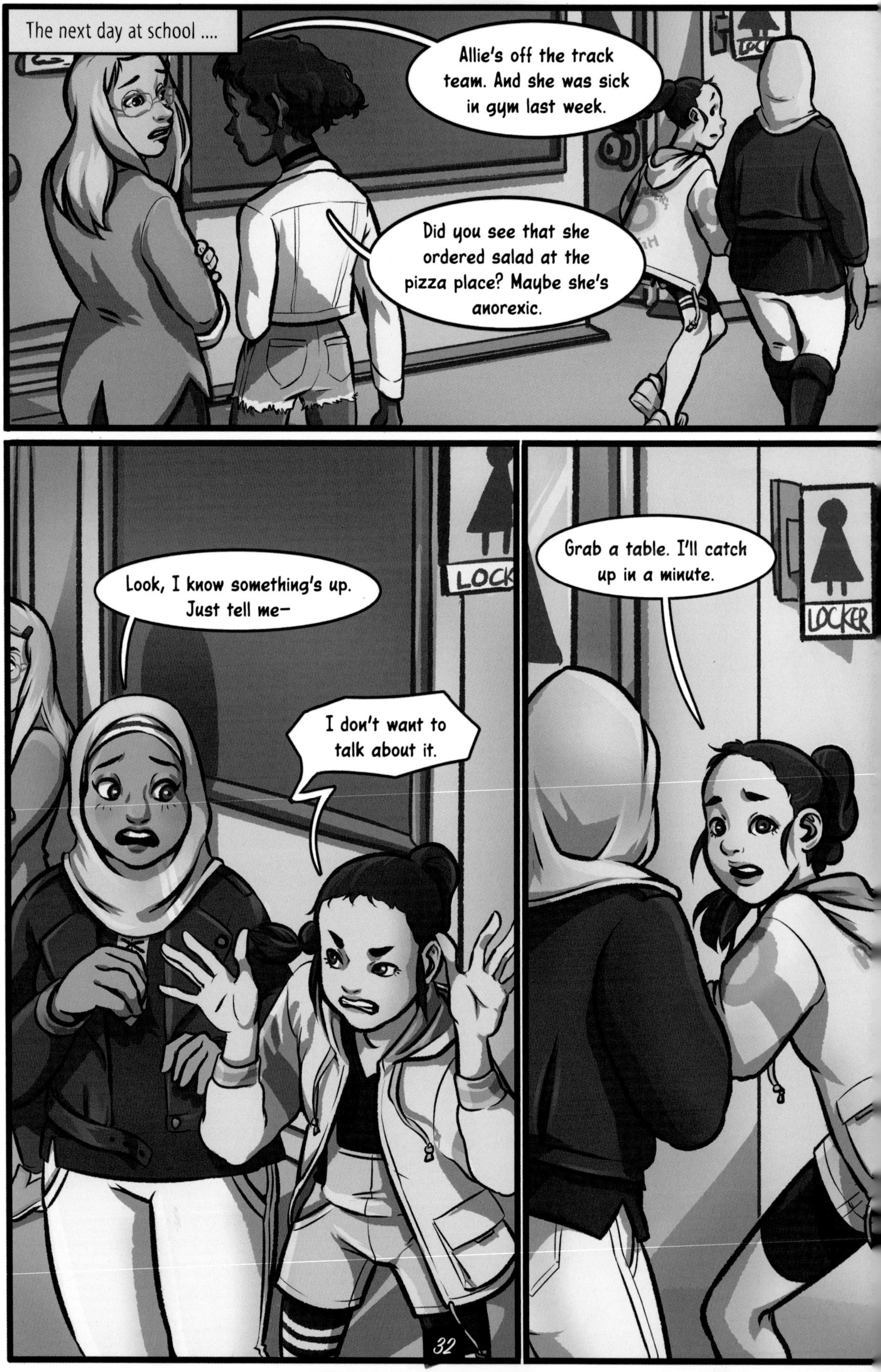

The next day at school ....
Allie's off the track team. And she was sick in gym last week.
Did you see that she ordered salad at the pizza place? Maybe she's anorexic.
Look, I know something's up. Just tell me—
I don't want to talk about it.
Grab a table. I'll catch up in a minute.
LOCKER

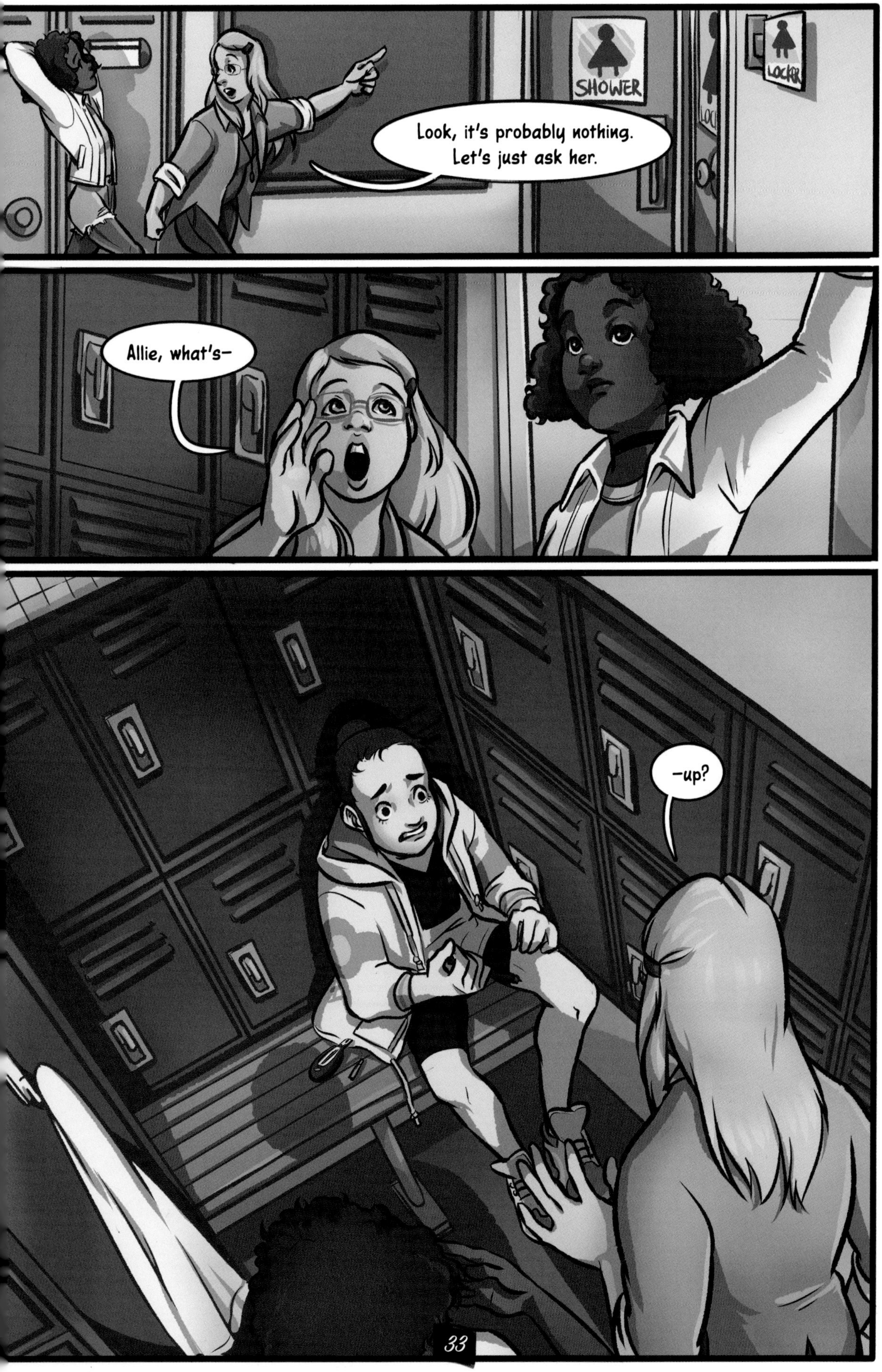
SHOWER
LOCKER
Look, it's probably nothing. Let's just ask her.
Allie, what's-
-up?

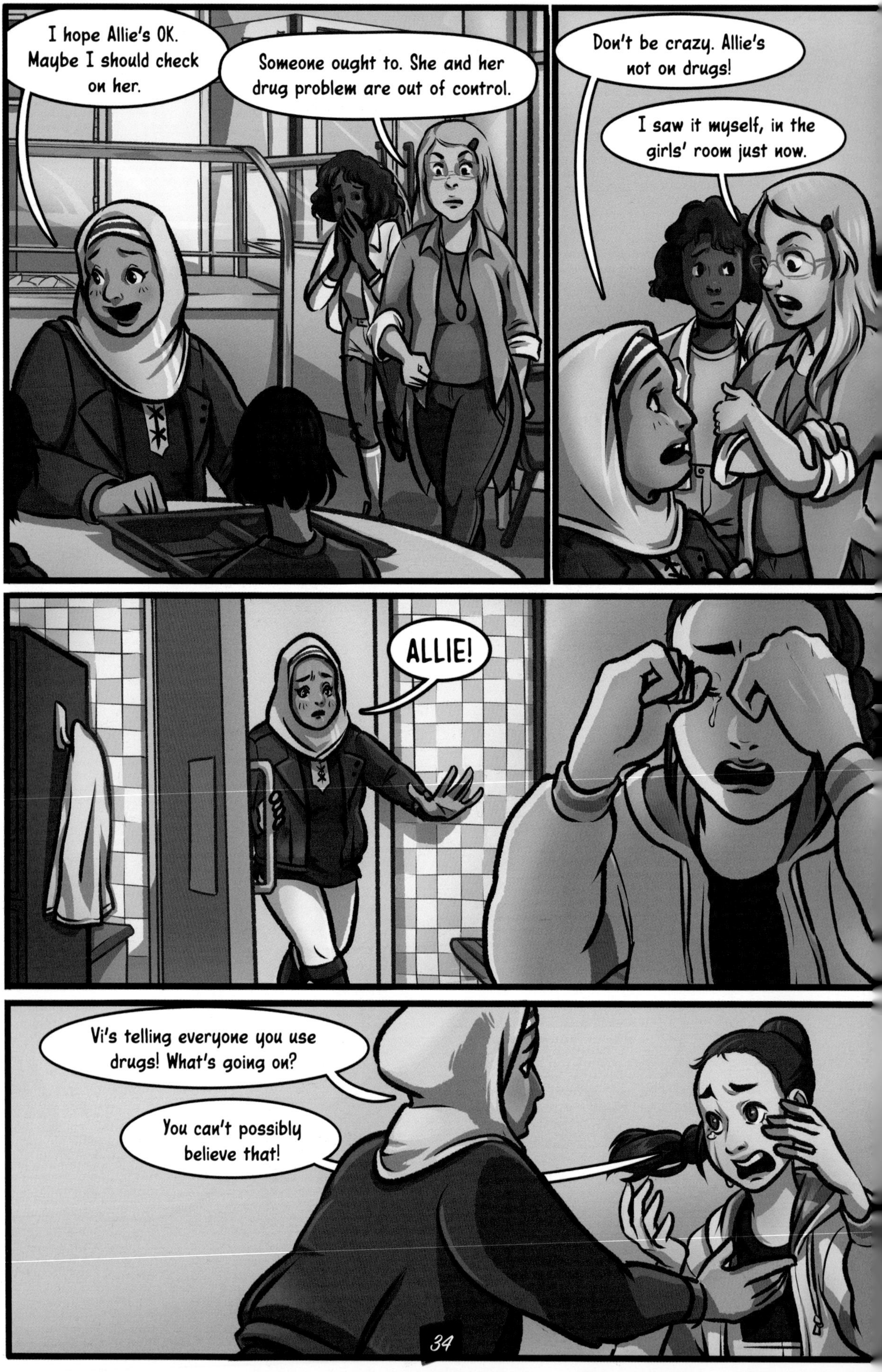
I hope Allie's OK. Maybe I should check on her.
Someone ought to. She and her drug problem are out of control.
Don't be crazy. Allie's not on drugs!
I saw it myself, in the girls' room just now.
ALLIE!
Vi's telling everyone you use drugs! What's going on?
You can't possibly believe that!

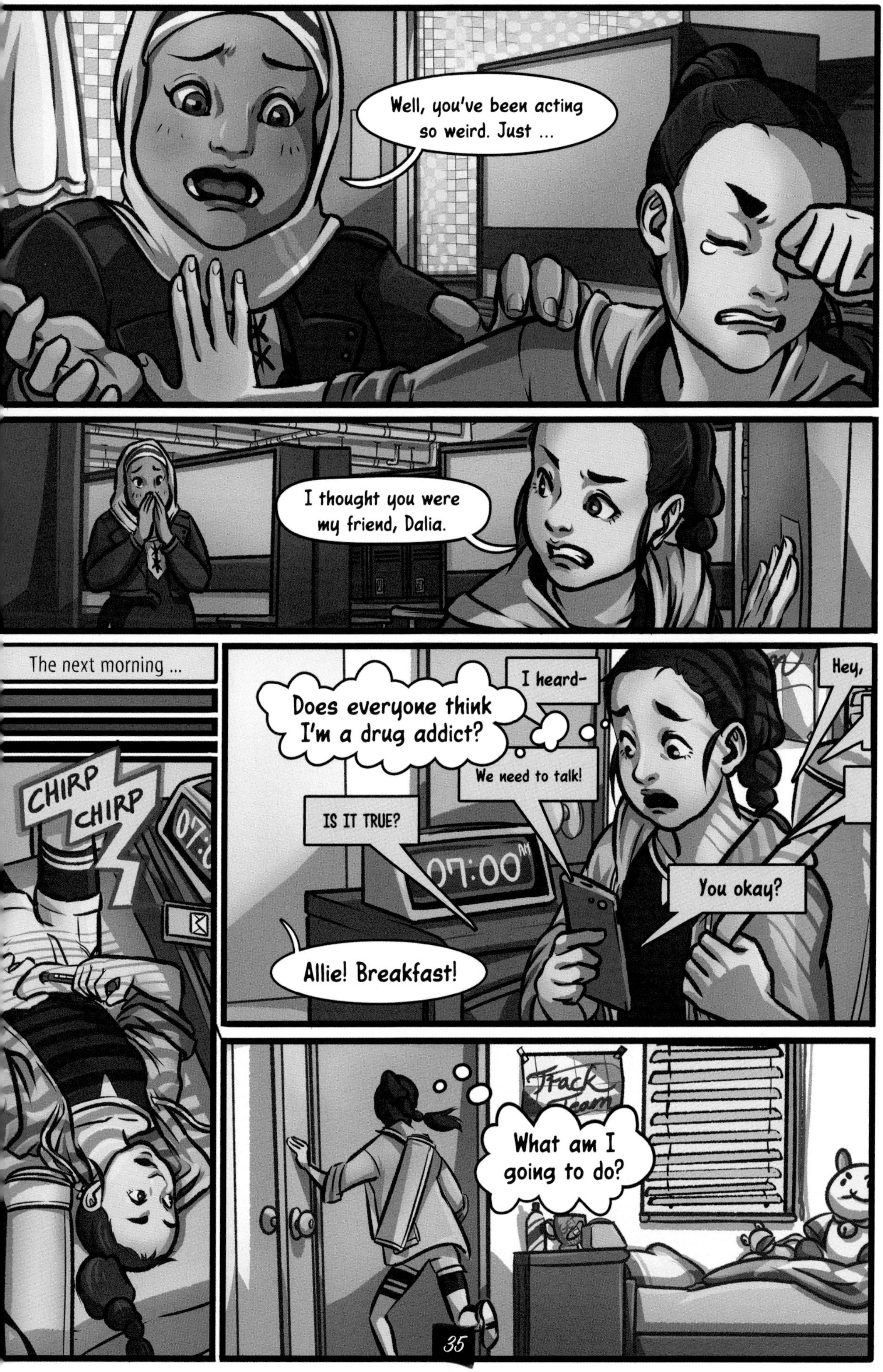

Well, you've been acting so weird. Just ...
I thought you were my friend, Dalia.
The next morning ...
CHIRP CHIRP
Does everyone think I'm a drug addict?
I heard-
We need to talk!
IS IT TRUE?
Hey,
You okay?
Allie! Breakfast!
What am I going to do?

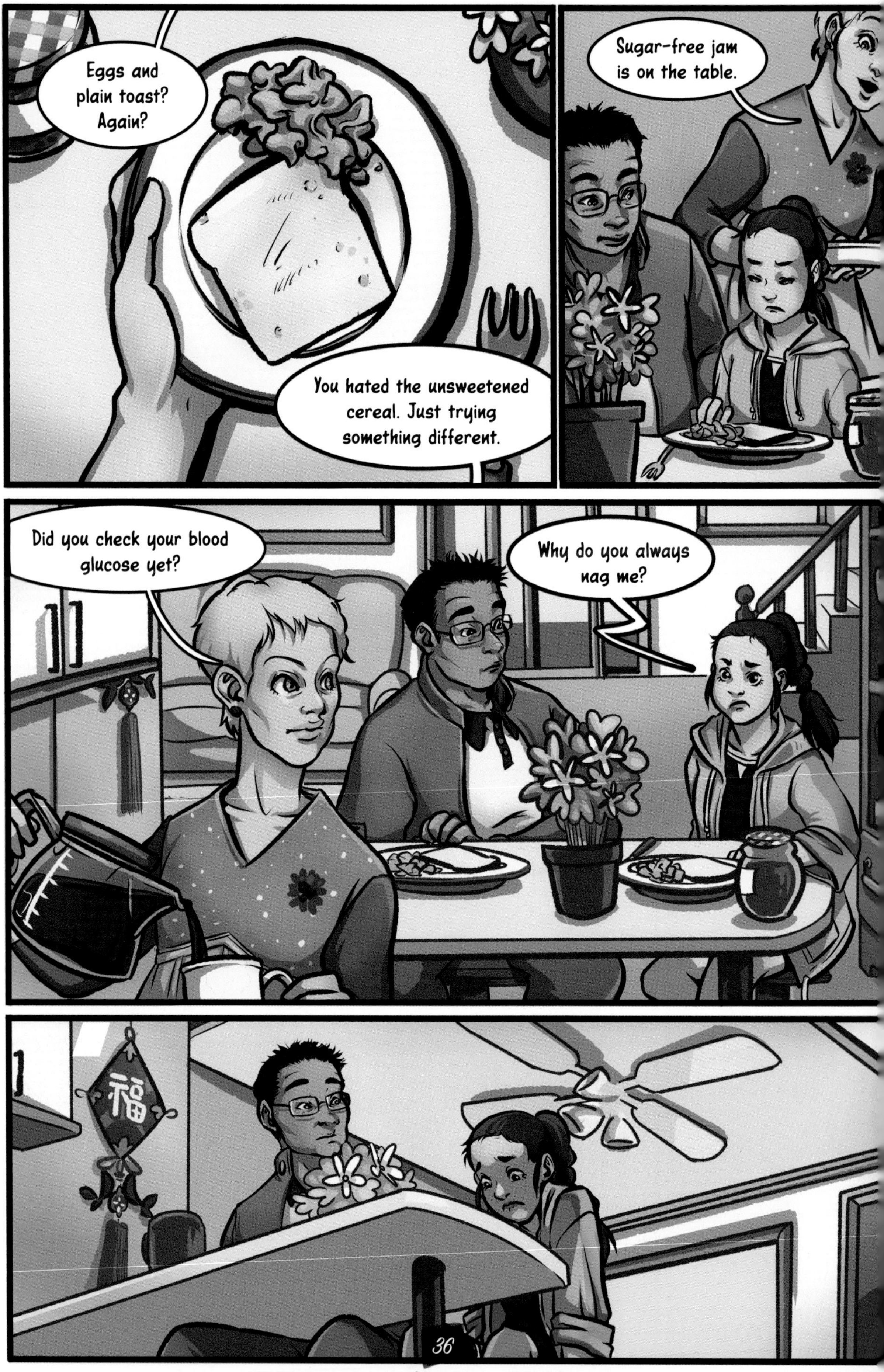
Eggs and plain toast? Again?
You hated the unsweetened cereal. Just trying something different.
Sugar-free jam is on the table.
Did you check your blood glucose yet?
Why do you always nag me?
福

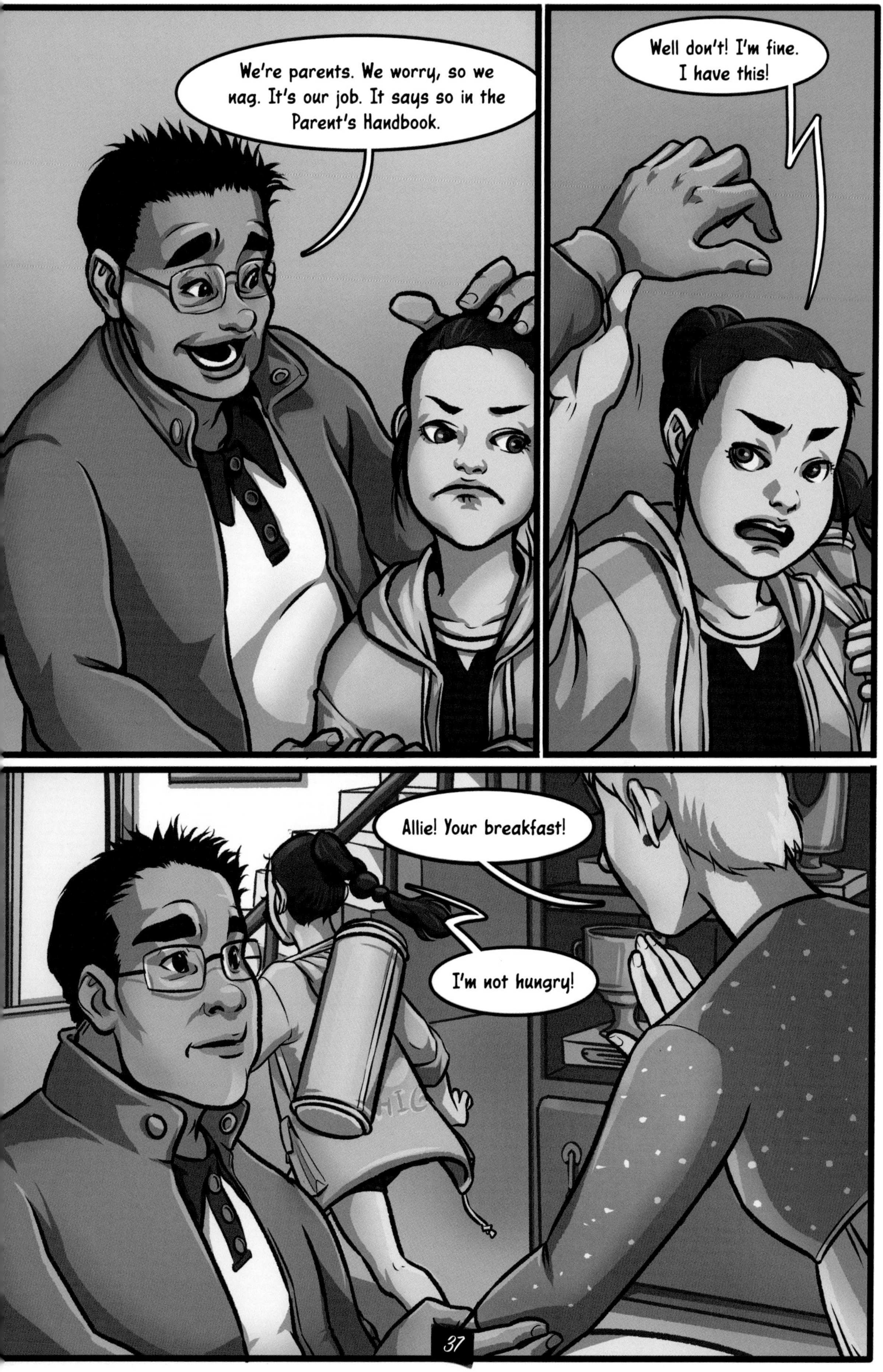
We're parents. We worry, so we nag. It's our job. It says so in the Parent's Handbook.
Well don't! I'm fine. I have this!
Allie! Your breakfast!
I'm not hungry!

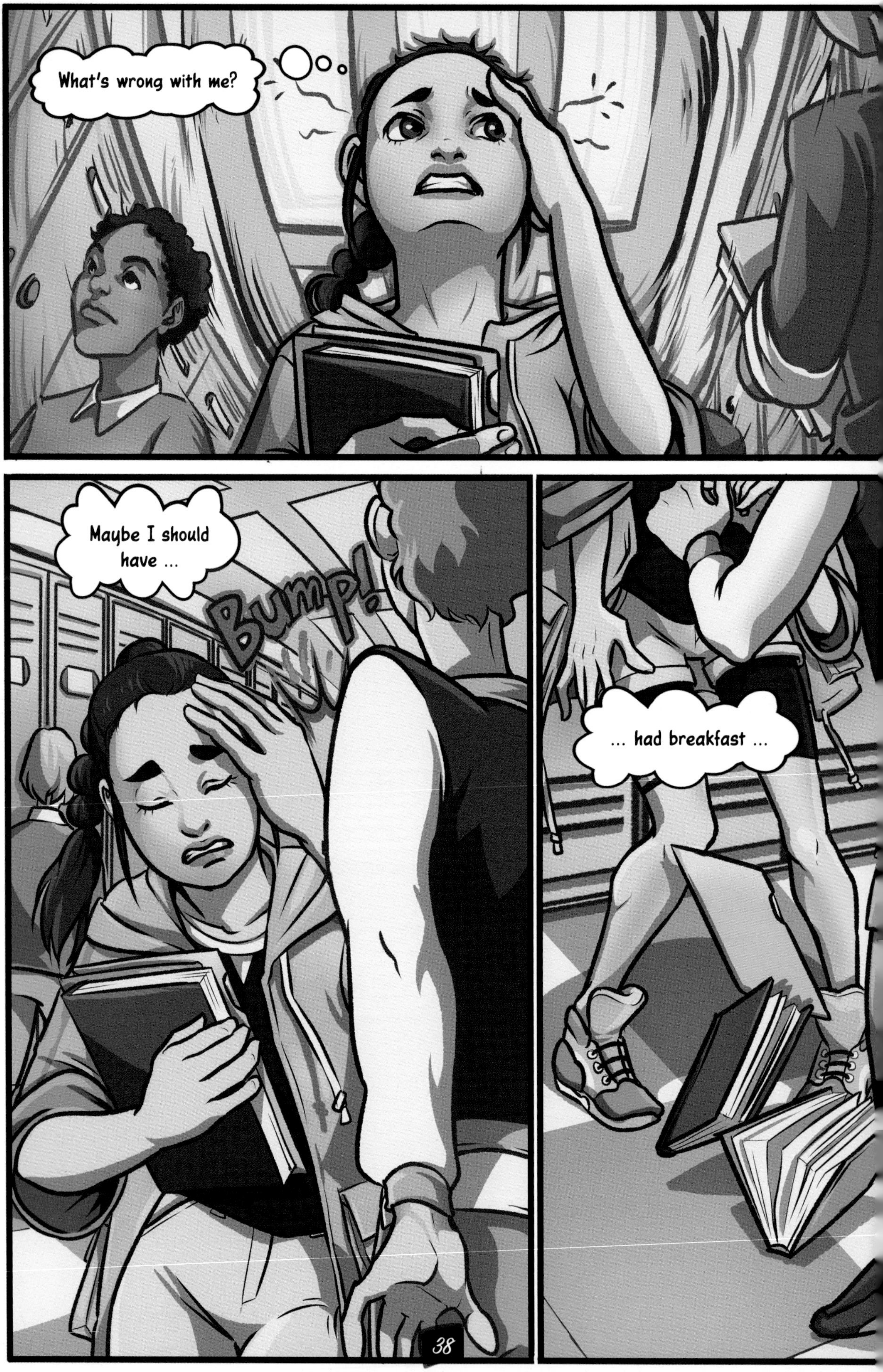
What's wrong with me?
Maybe I should have ...
Bump!
... had breakfast ...

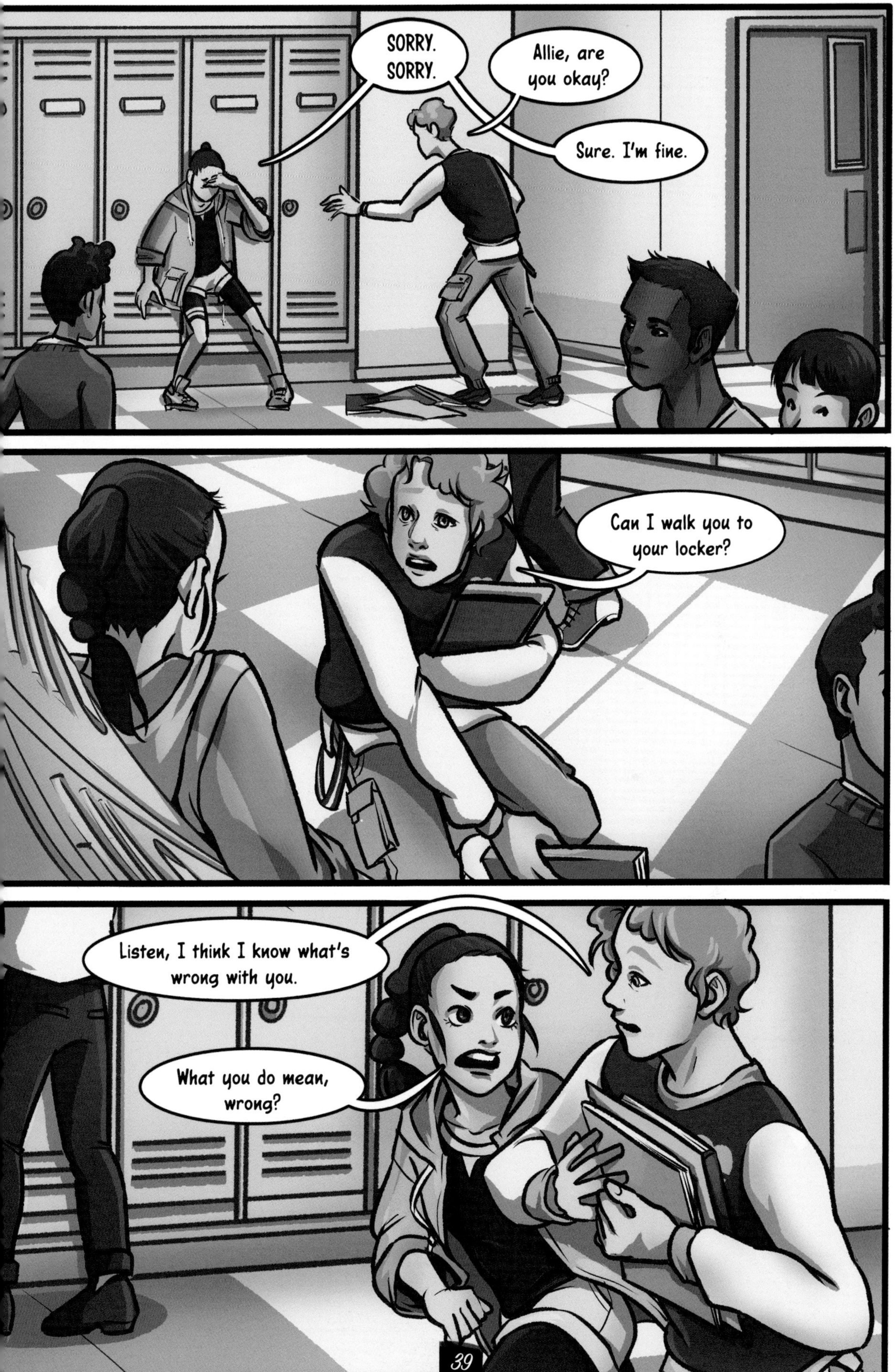
SORRY. SORRY.
Allie, are you okay?
Sure. I'm fine.
Can I walk you to your locker?
Listen, I think I know what's wrong with you.
What you do mean, wrong?

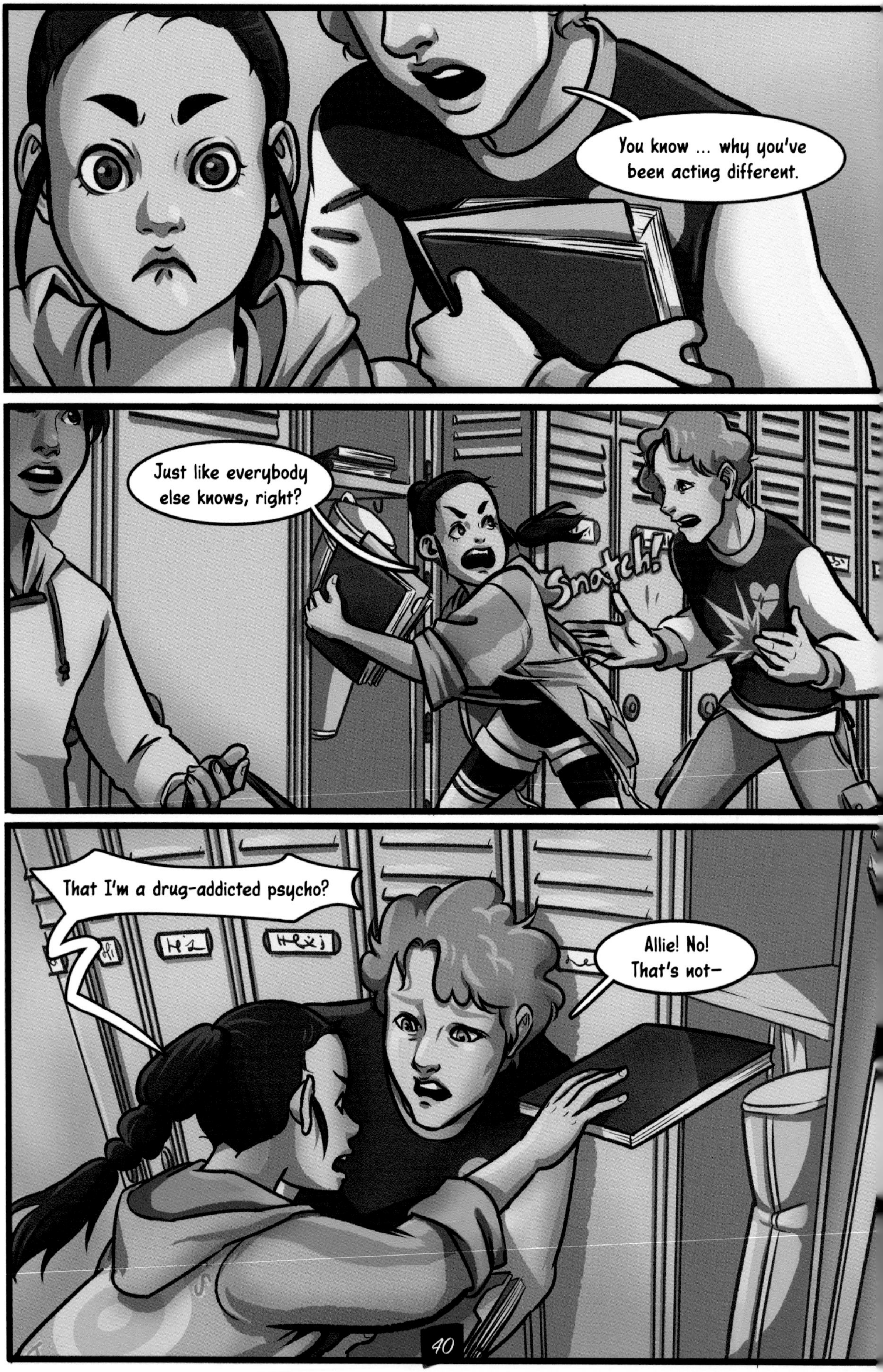

You know ... why you've been acting different.
Just like everybody else knows, right?
Snatch!
That I'm a drug-addicted psycho?
Allie! No! That's not–

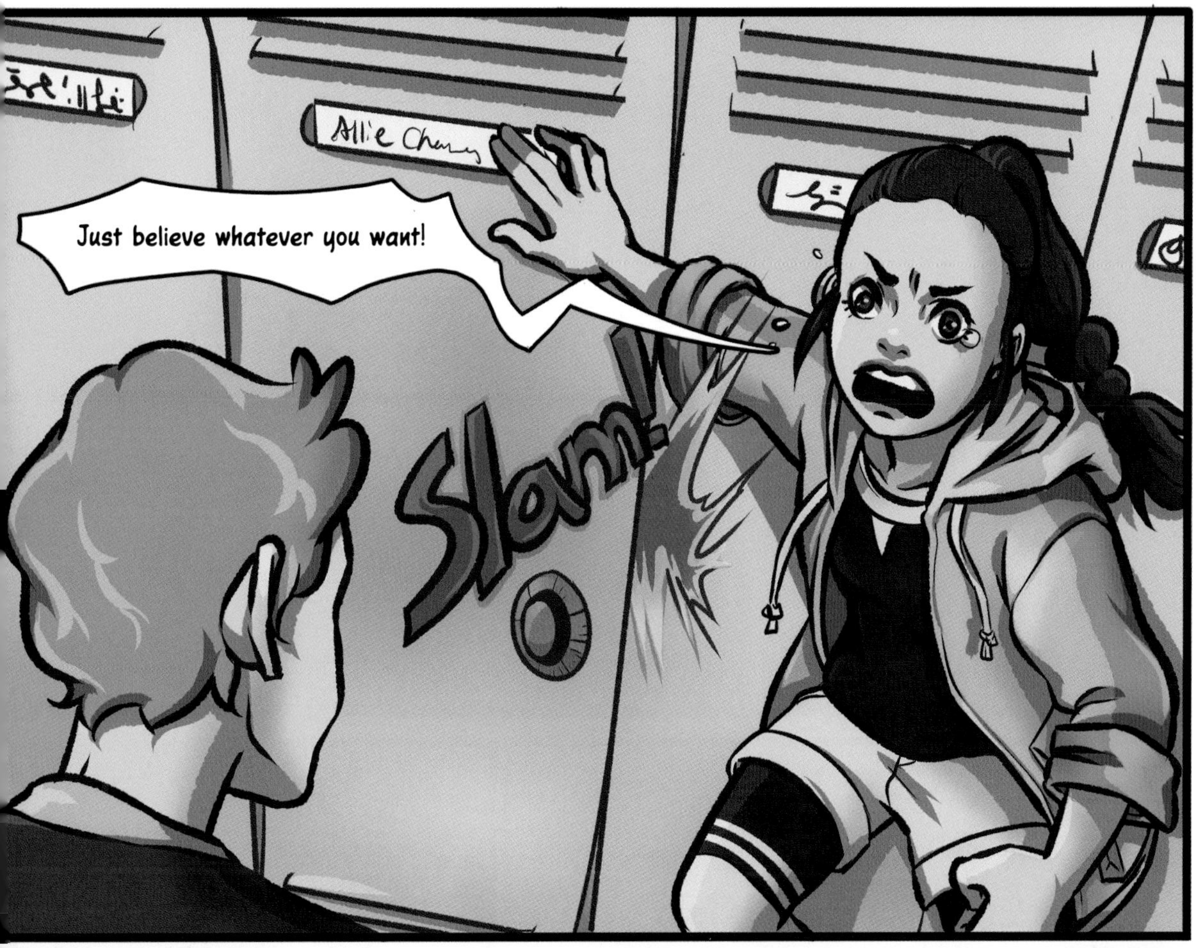
Just believe whatever you want!
Slam!

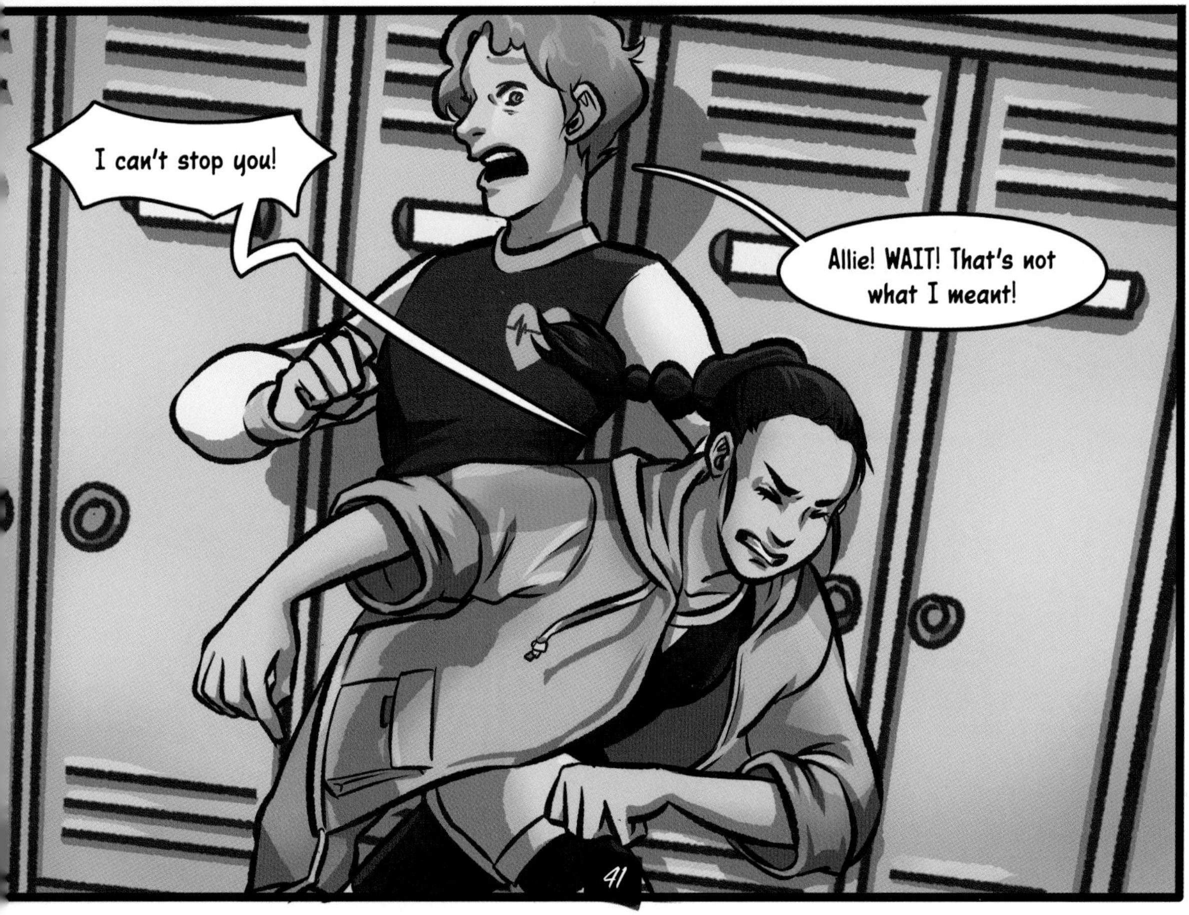
I can't stop you!
Allie! WAIT! That's not what I meant!

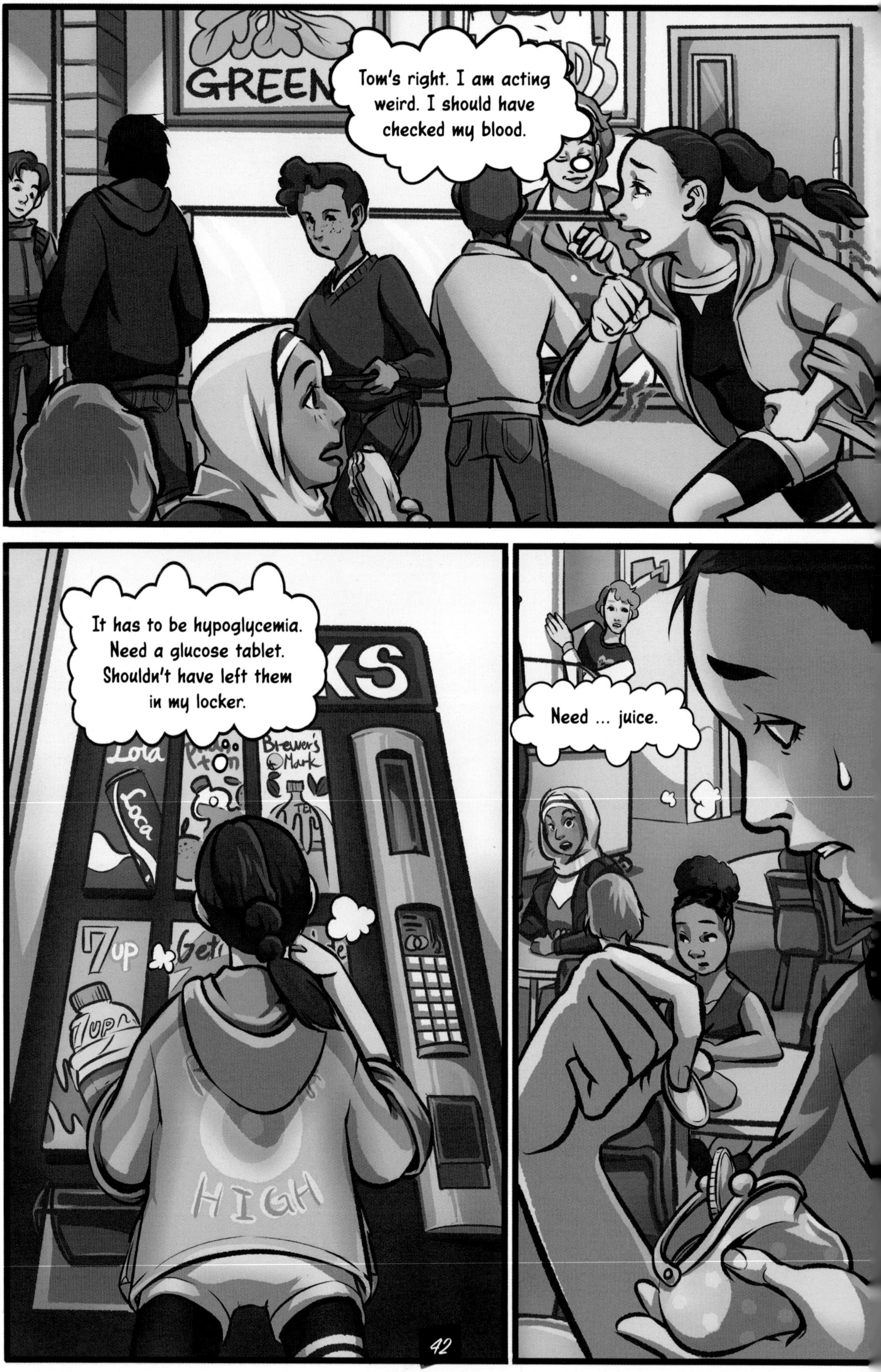
GREEN
Tom's right. I am acting weird. I should have checked my blood.
It has to be hypoglycemia. Need a glucose tablet. Shouldn't have left them in my locker.
KS
Lola
Loca
Brewer's Mark
7up
HIGH
Need ... juice.

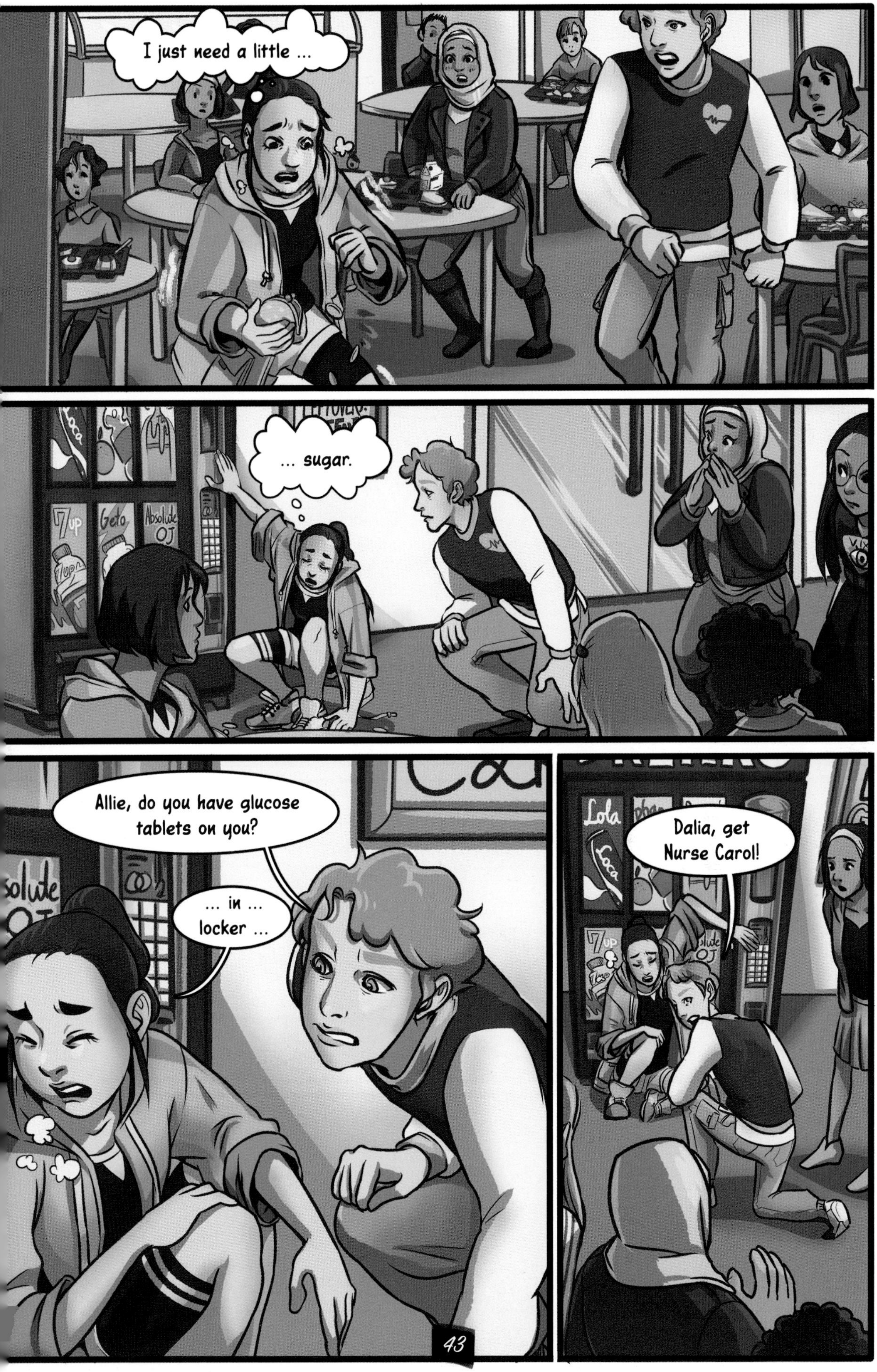
I just need a little ...
... sugar.
7up
Geto
Absolute OJ
Allie, do you have glucose tablets on you?
... in ... locker ...
Lola
Loca
Dalia, get Nurse Carol!

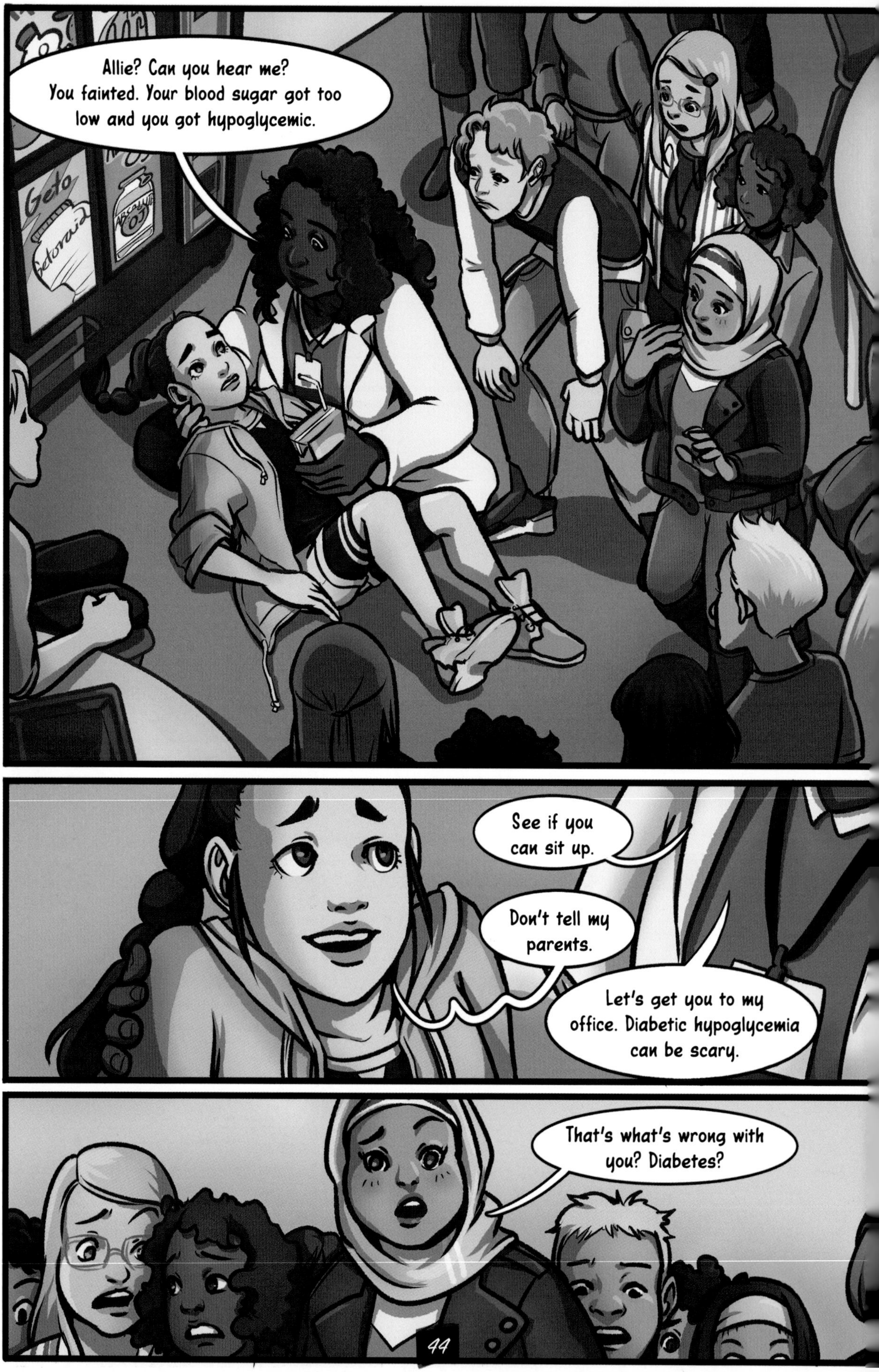
Allie? Can you hear me? You fainted. Your blood sugar got too low and you got hypoglycemic.
Gatorade
See if you can sit up.
Don't tell my parents.
Let's get you to my office. Diabetic hypoglycemia can be scary.
That's what's wrong with you? Diabetes?

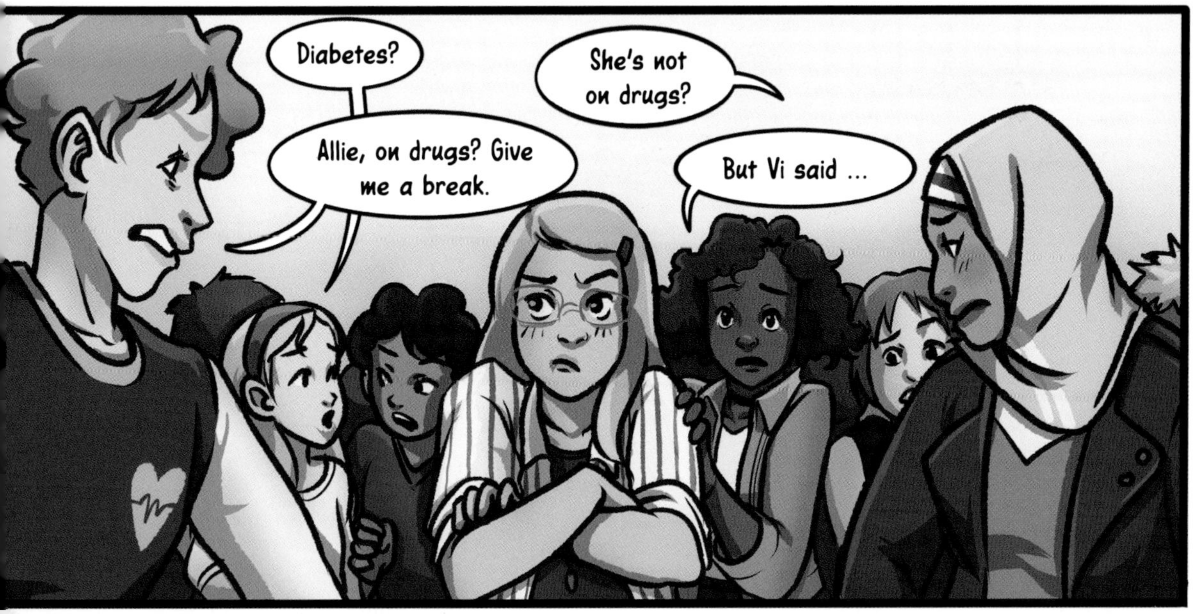
Diabetes?
Allie, on drugs? Give me a break.
She's not on drugs?
But Vi said ...

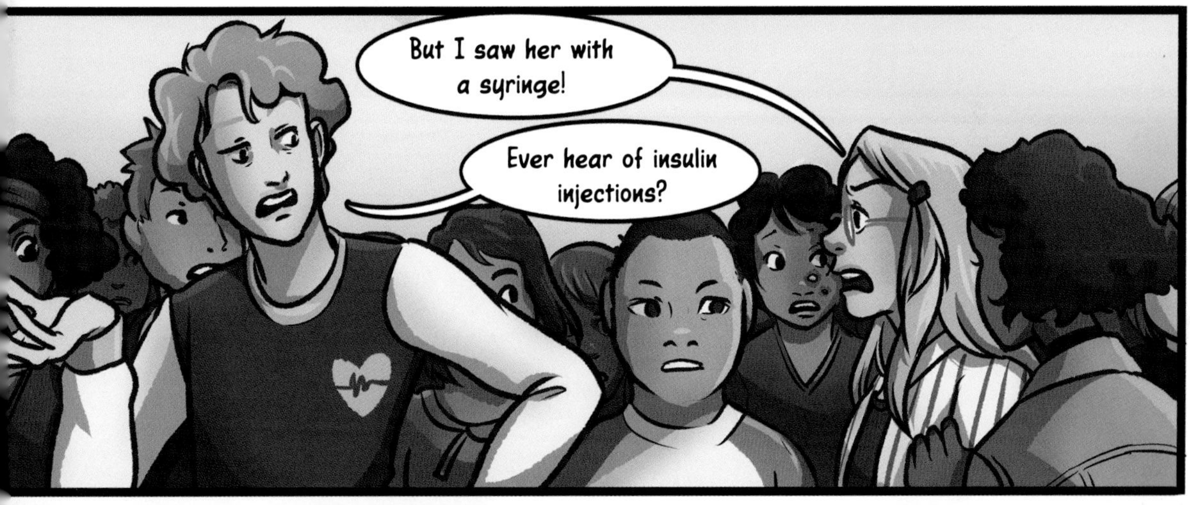
But I saw her with a syringe!
Ever hear of insulin injections?

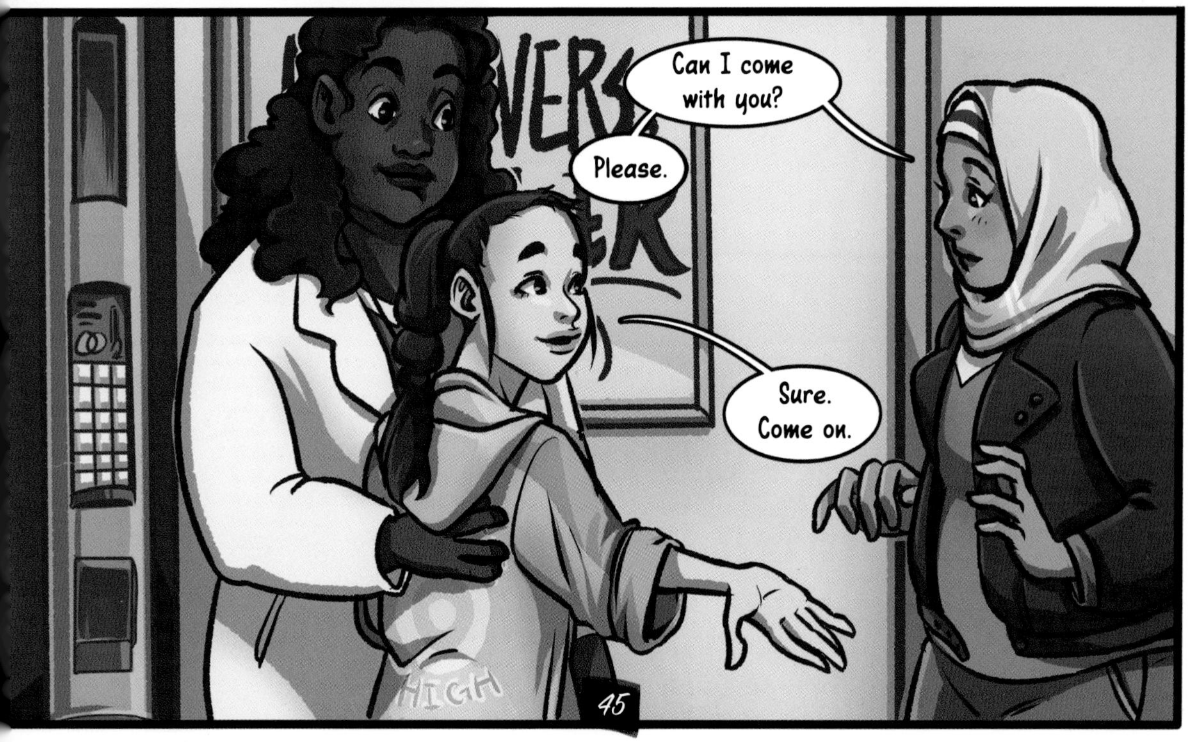
Can I come with you?
Please.
Sure. Come on.
HIGH

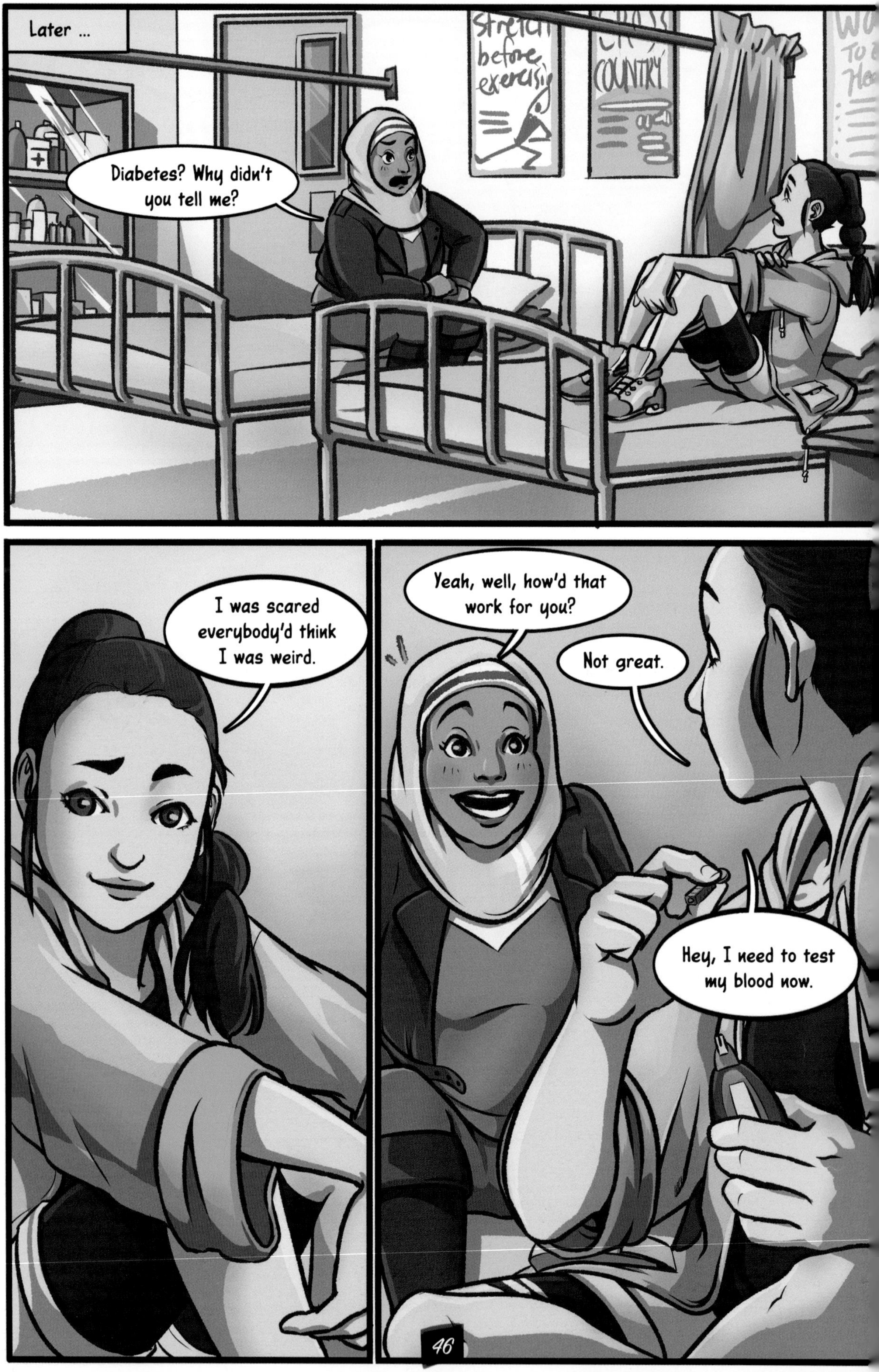

Later ...
Diabetes? Why didn't you tell me?
I was scared everybody'd think I was weird.
Yeah, well, how'd that work for you?
Not great.
Hey, I need to test my blood now.

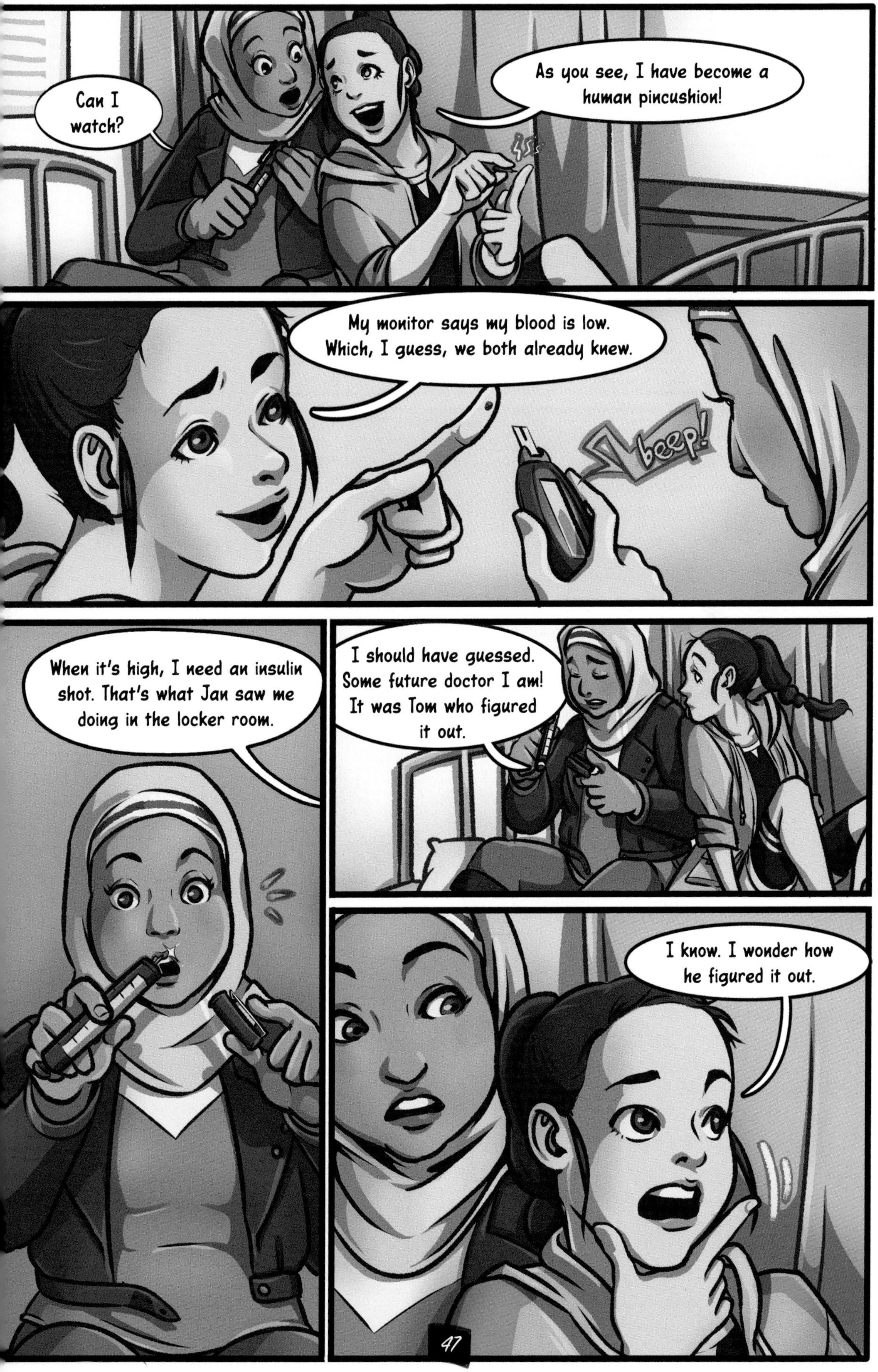
Can I watch?
As you see, I have become a human pincushion!
My monitor says my blood is low. Which, I guess, we both already knew.
beep!
When it's high, I need an insulin shot. That's what Jan saw me doing in the locker room.
I should have guessed. Some future doctor I am! It was Tom who figured it out.
I know. I wonder how he figured it out.

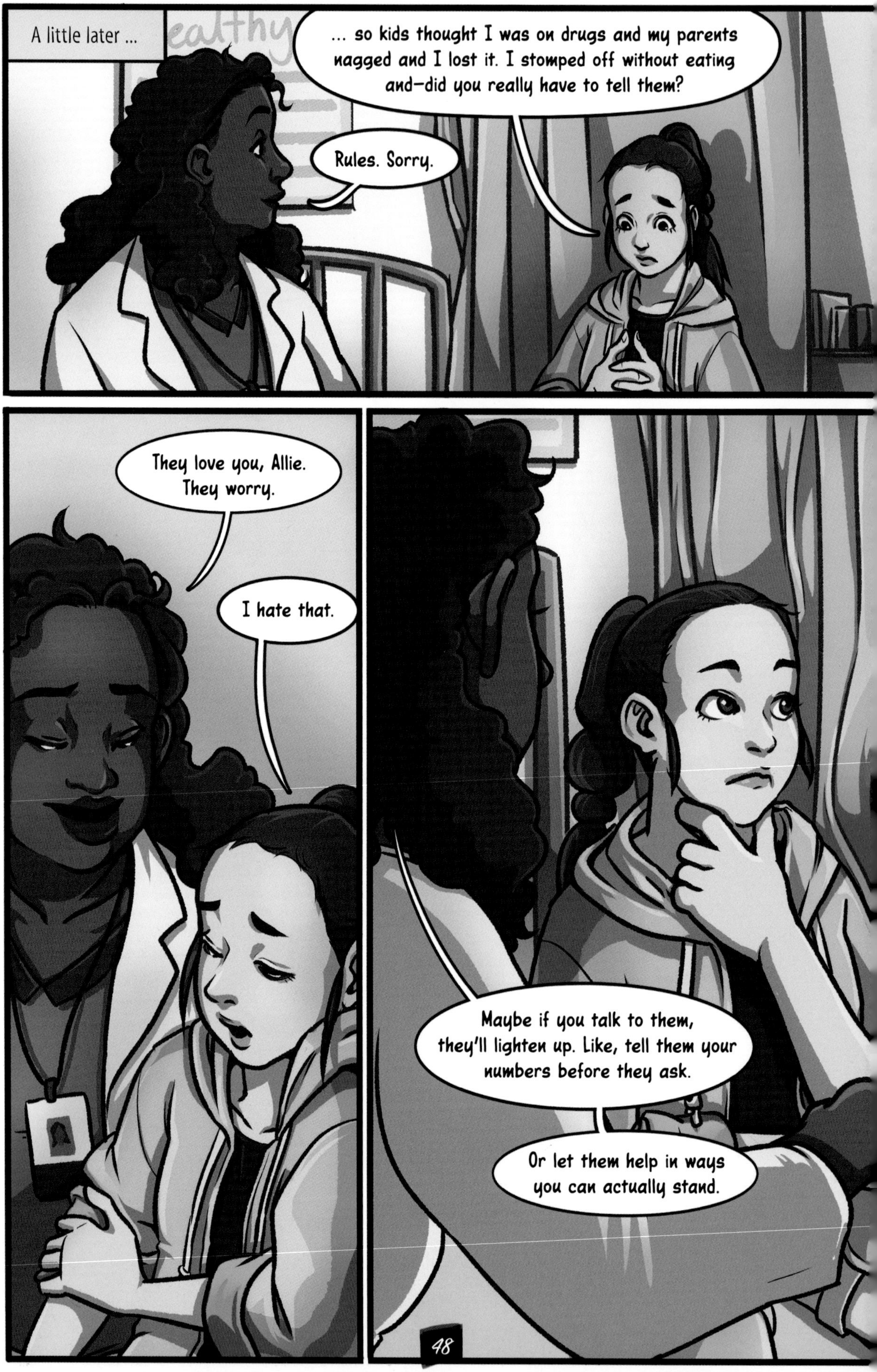
A little later ...
... so kids thought I was on drugs and my parents nagged and I lost it. I stomped off without eating and—did you really have to tell them?
Rules. Sorry.
They love you, Allie. They worry.
I hate that.
Maybe if you talk to them, they'll lighten up. Like, tell them your numbers before they ask.
Or let them help in ways you can actually stand.

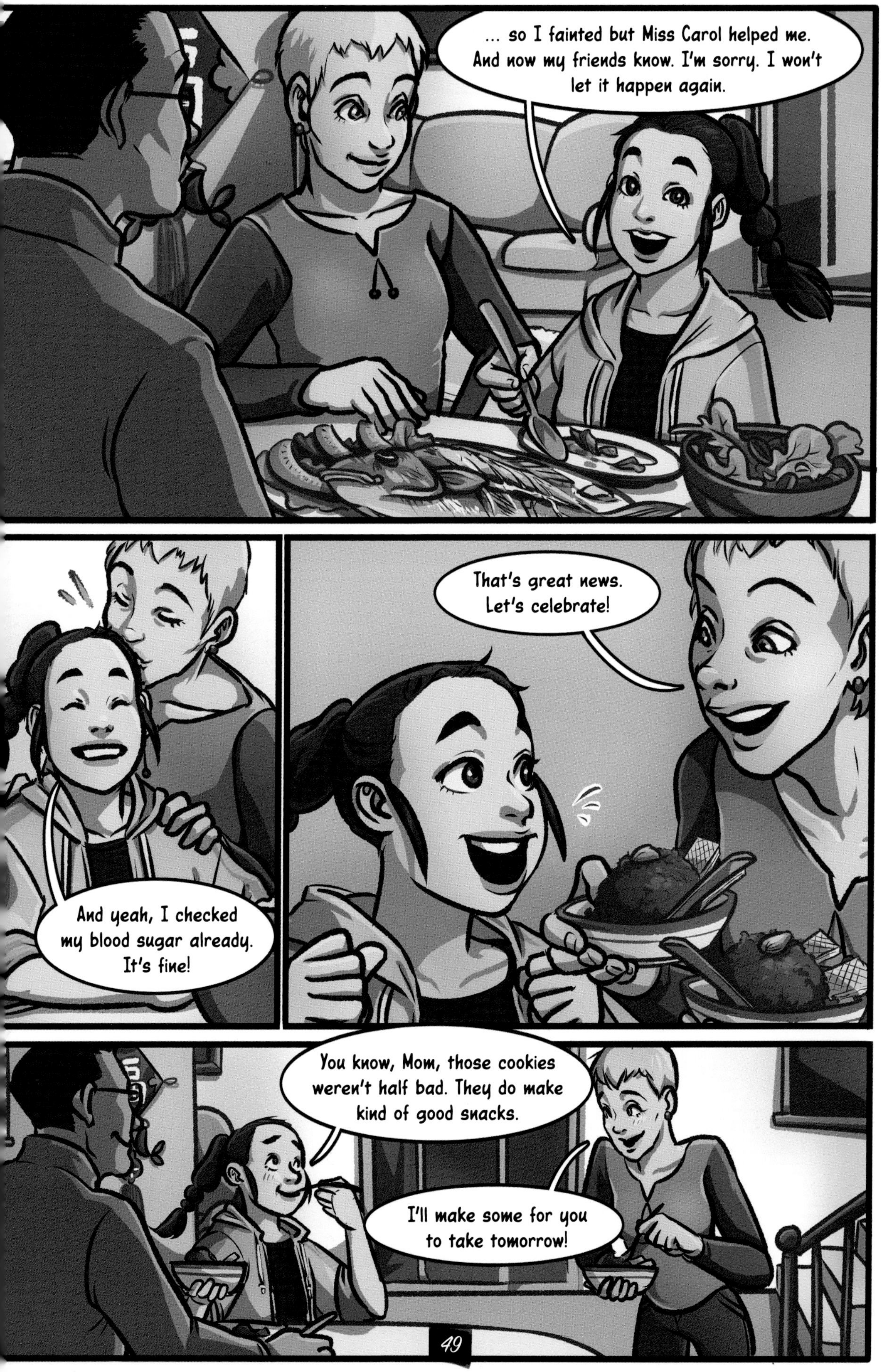

... so I fainted but Miss Carol helped me. And now my friends know. I'm sorry. I won't let it happen again.
And yeah, I checked my blood sugar already. It's fine!
That's great news. Let's celebrate!
You know, Mom, those cookies weren't half bad. They do make kind of good snacks.
I'll make some for you to take tomorrow!

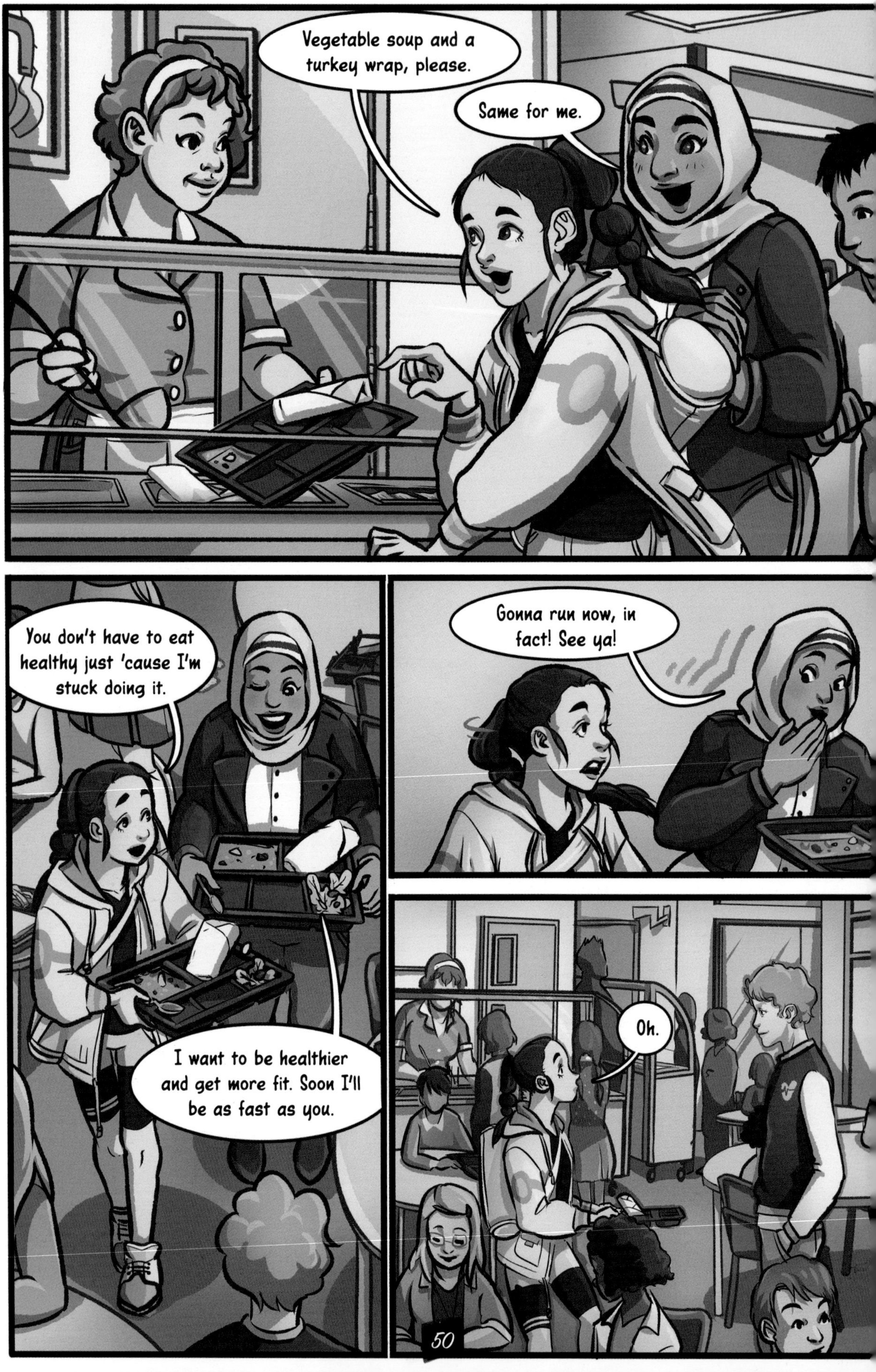
Vegetable soup and a turkey wrap, please.
Same for me.
You don't have to eat healthy just 'cause I'm stuck doing it.
I want to be healthier and get more fit. Soon I'll be as fast as you.
Gonna run now, in fact! See ya!
Oh.

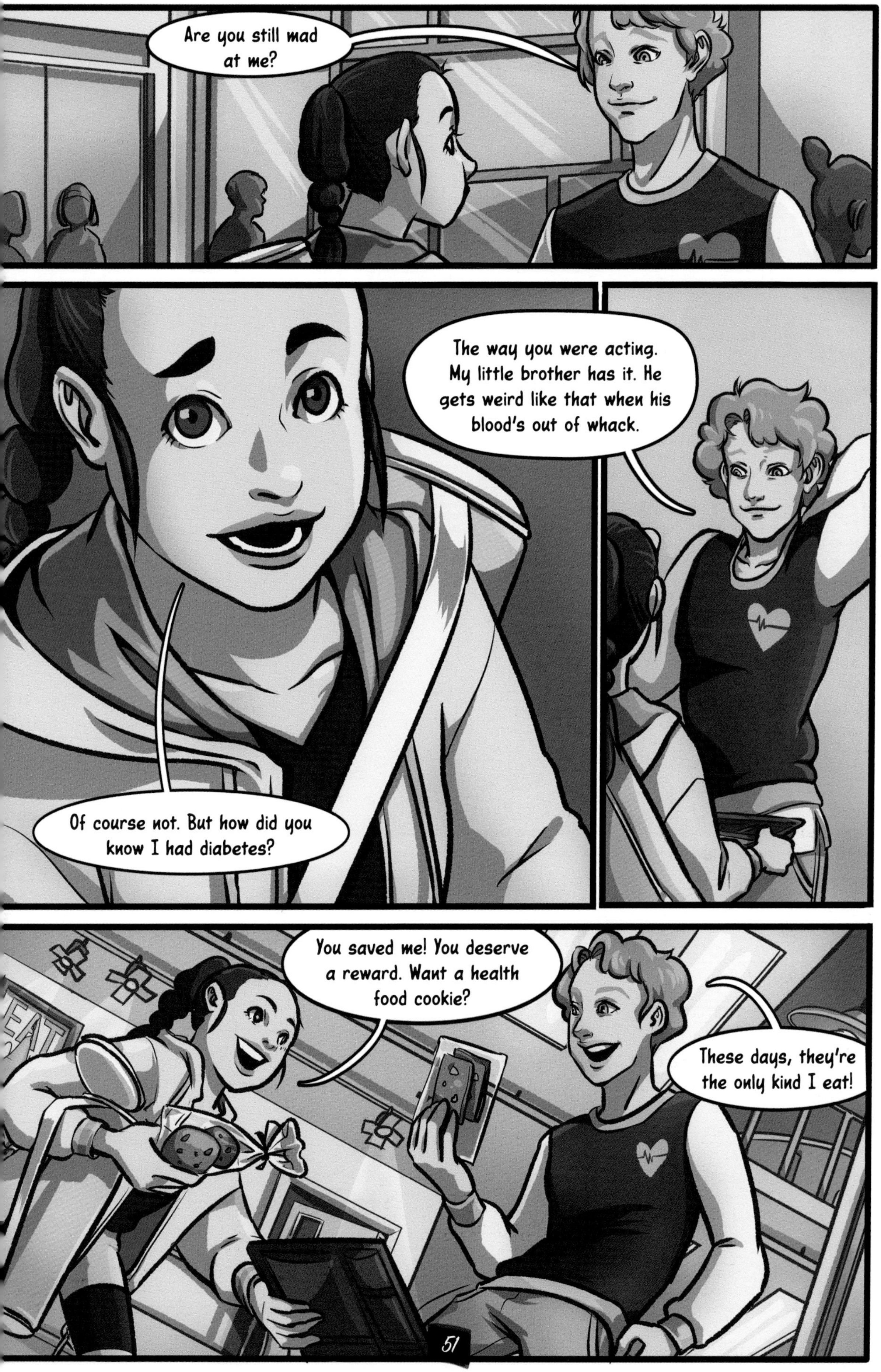
Are you still mad at me?
Of course not. But how did you know I had diabetes?
The way you were acting. My little brother has it. He gets weird like that when his blood's out of whack.
You saved me! You deserve a reward. Want a health food cookie?
These days, they're the only kind I eat!
EAT

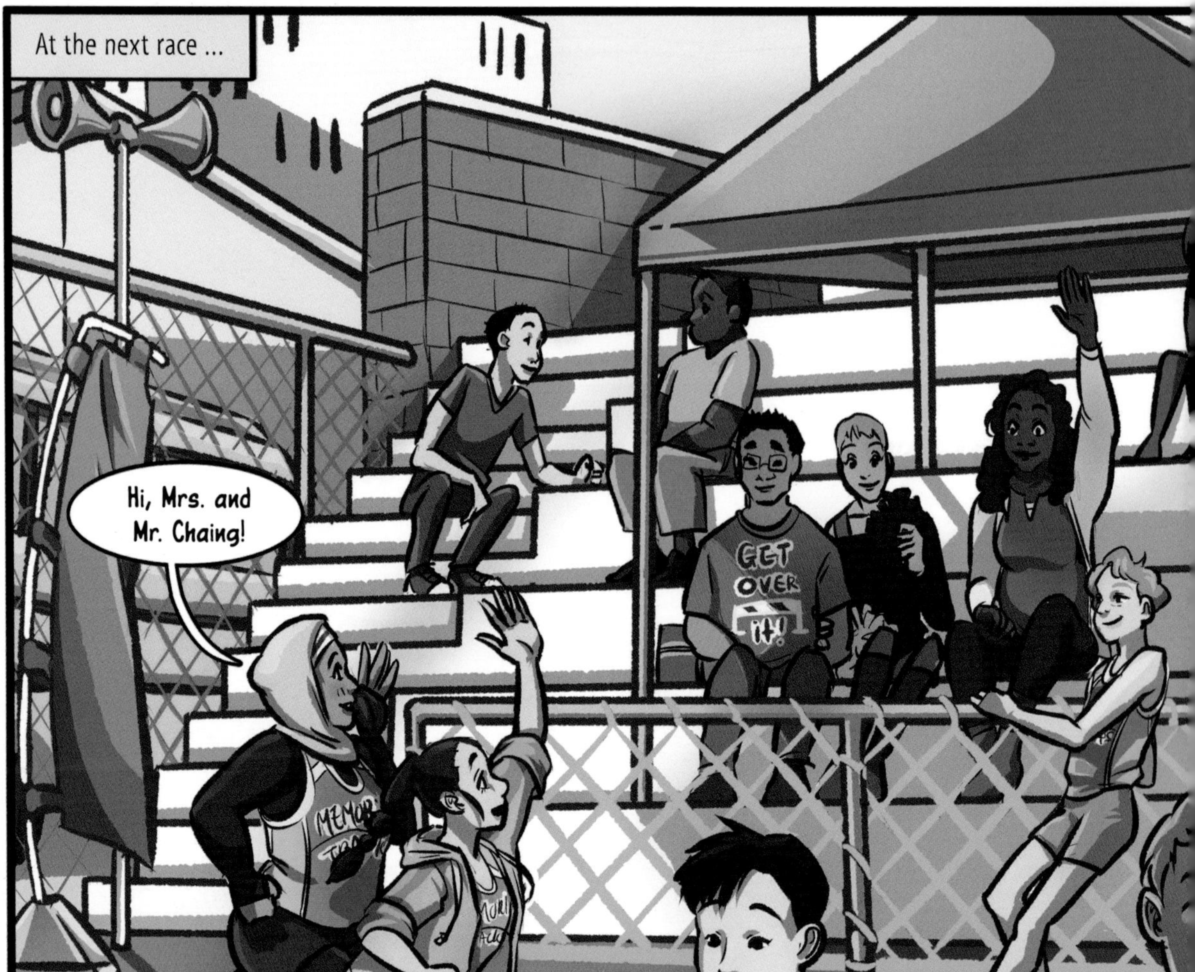
At the next race ...
Hi, Mrs. and Mr. Chaing!
GET OVER it!

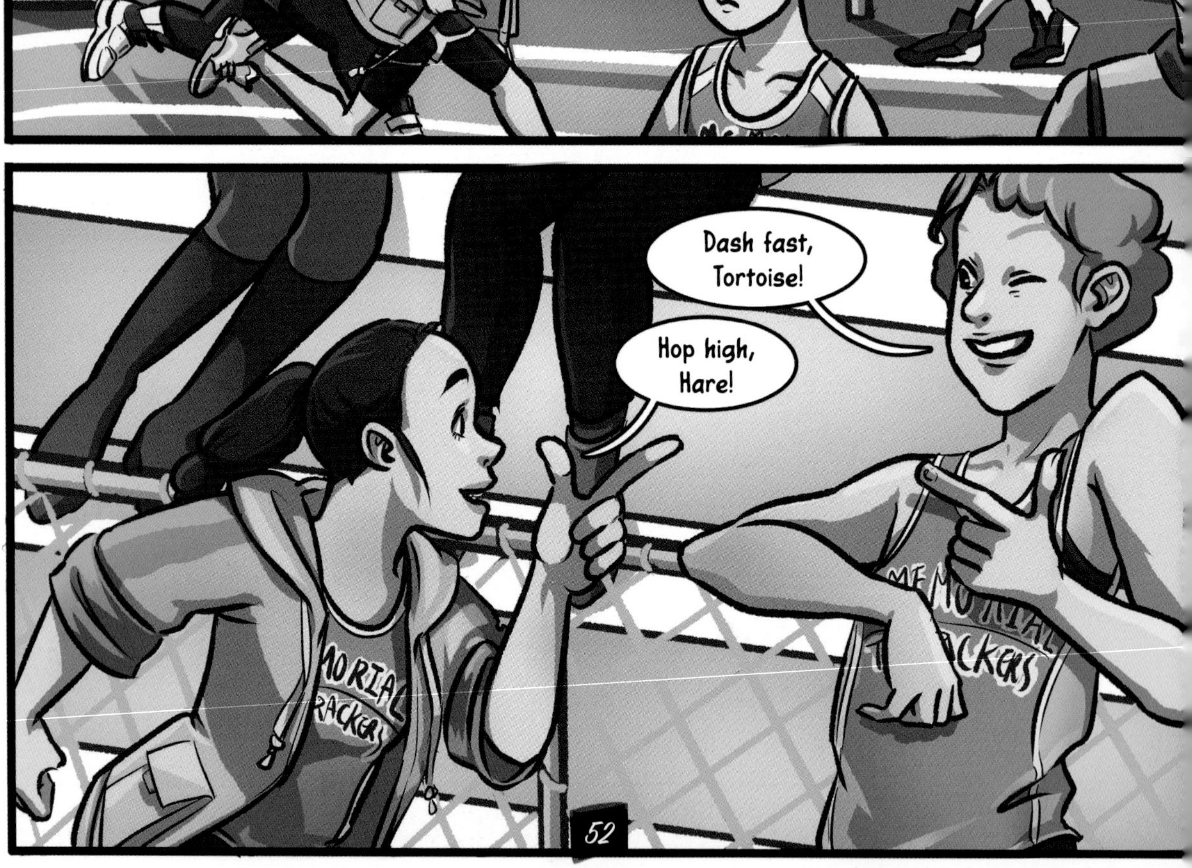
Dash fast, Tortoise!
Hop high, Hare!
MEMORIAL TRACKERS

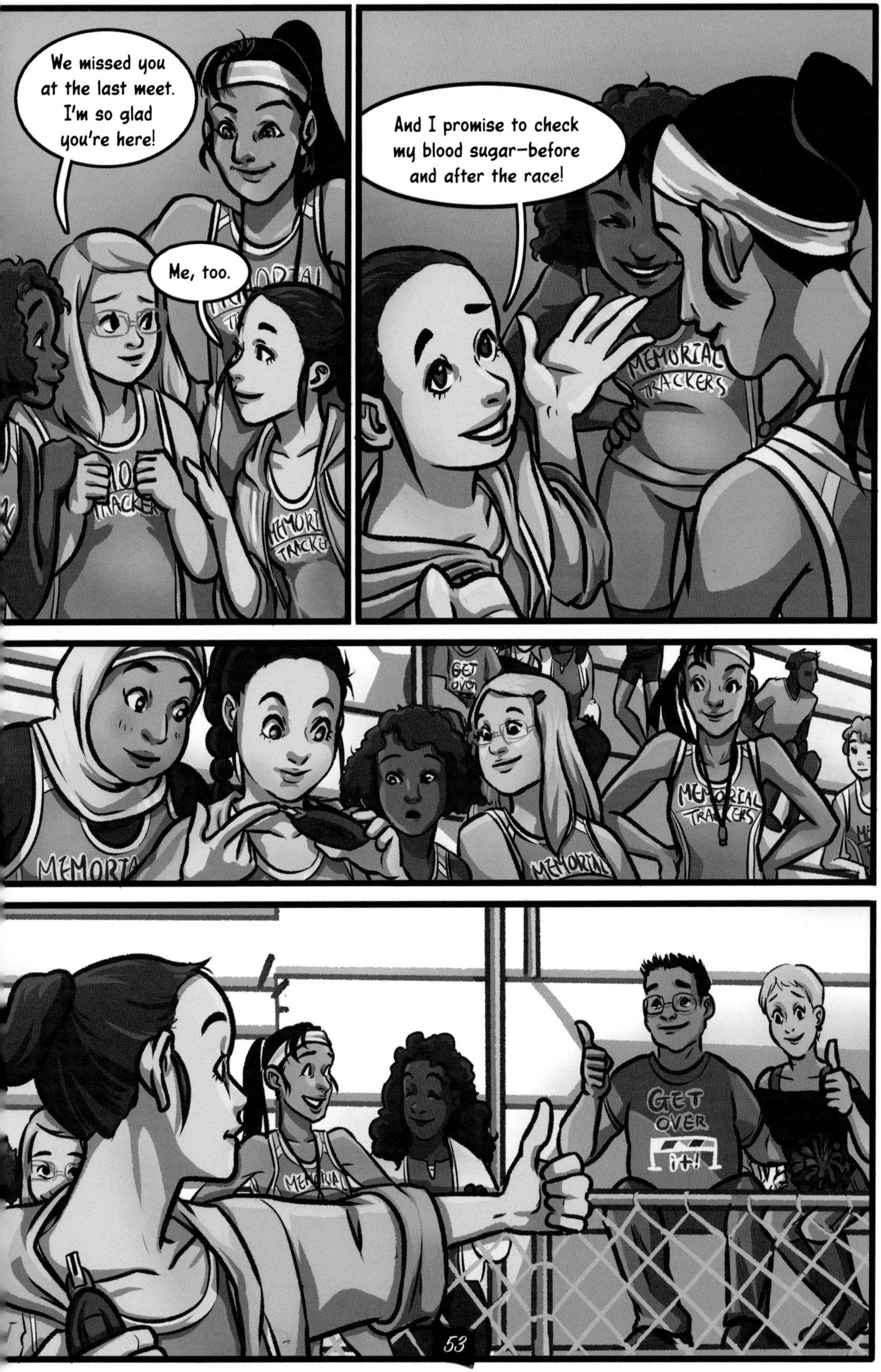
We missed you at the last meet. I'm so glad you're here!
Me, too.
MEMORIAL TRACKERS
And I promise to check my blood sugar—before and after the race!
MEMORIAL TRACKERS
GET OVER
MEMORIAL TRACKERS
MEMORIAL
GET OVER IT!

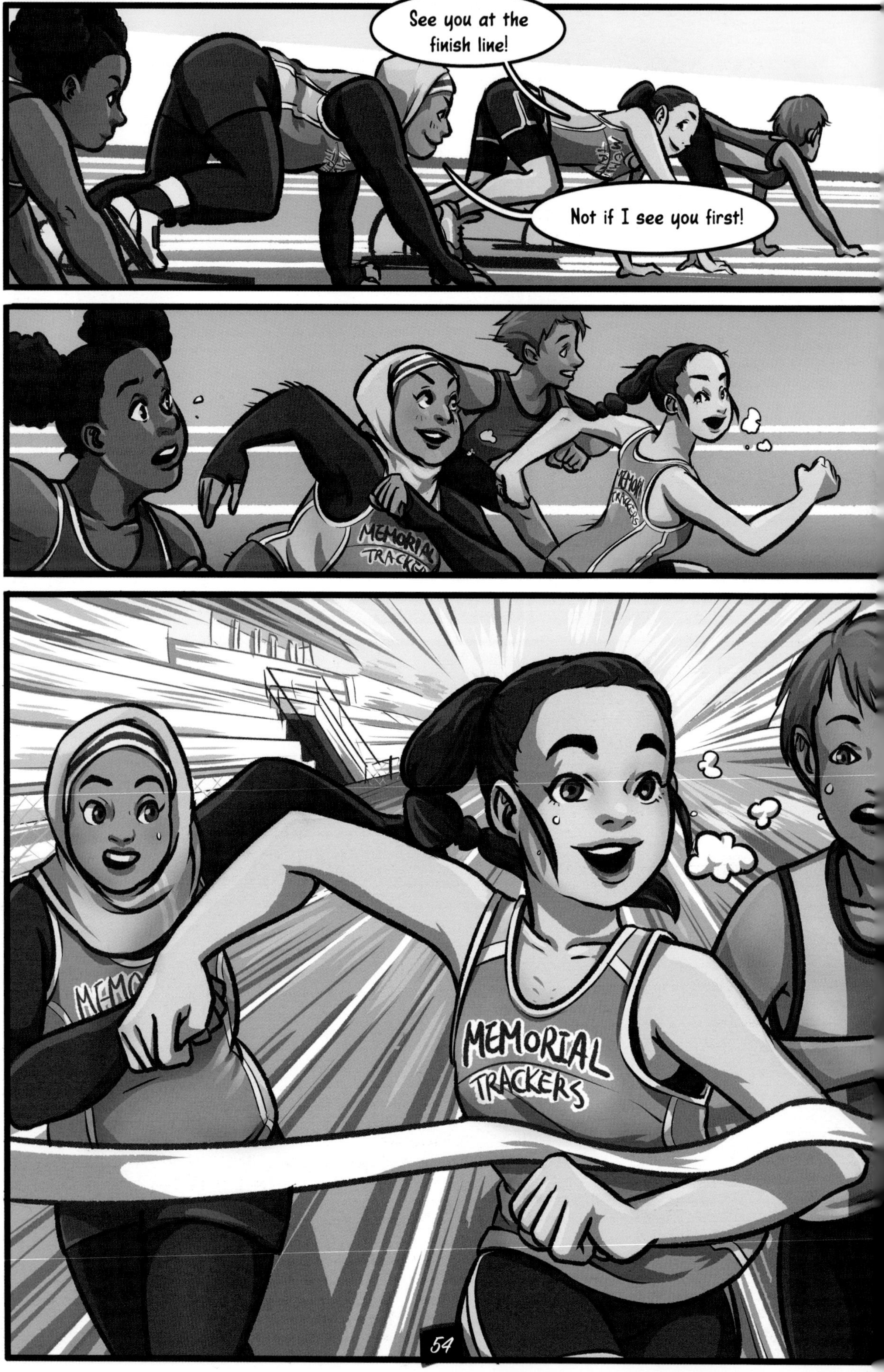
See you at the finish line!
Not if I see you first!
MEMORIAL TRACKERS

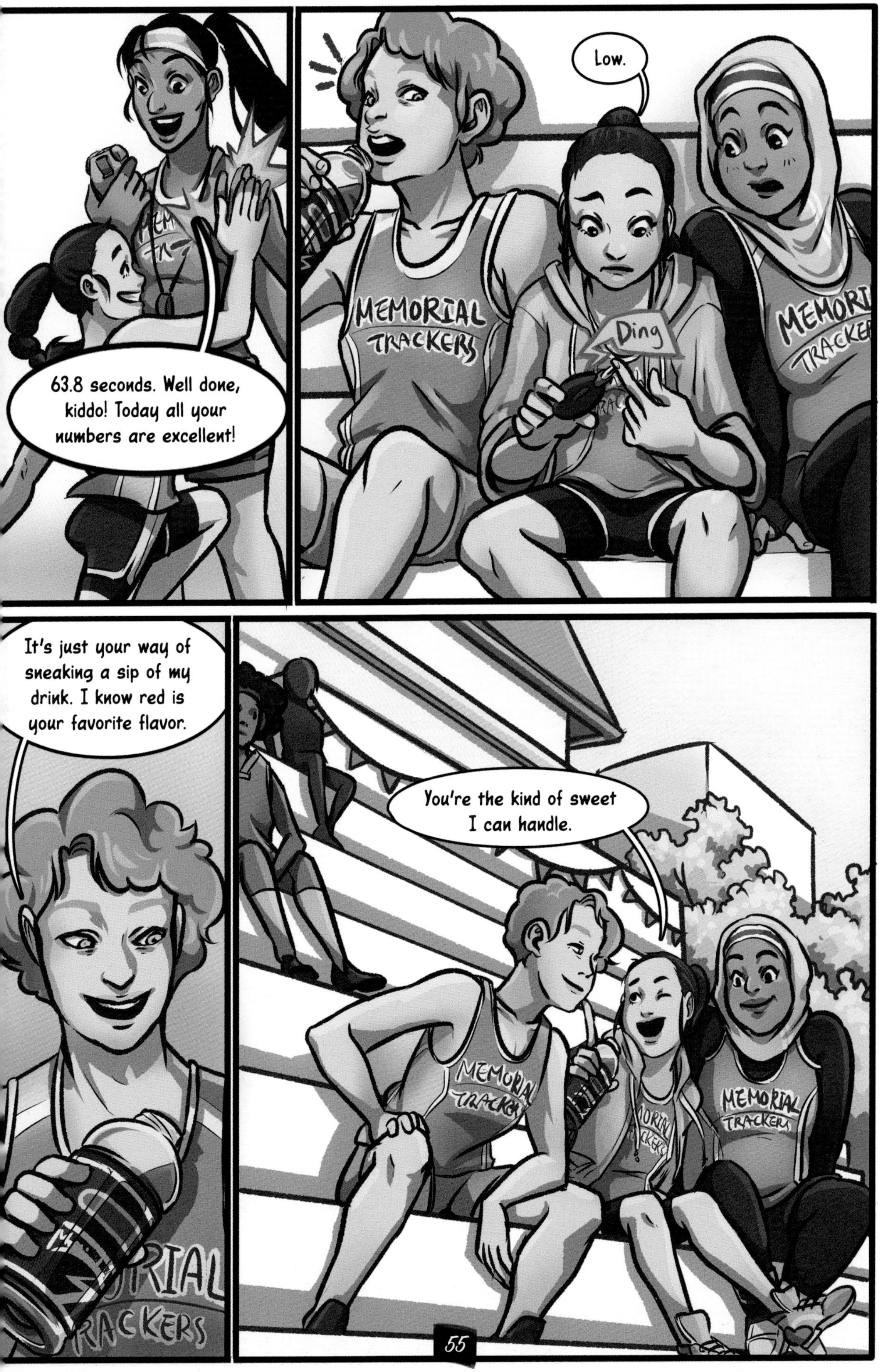
63.8 seconds. Well done, kiddo! Today all your numbers are excellent!
MEMORIAL TRACKERS
Low.
Ding
MEMORIAL TRACKERS
It's just your way of sneaking a sip of my drink. I know red is your favorite flavor.
RIAL TRACKERS
You're the kind of sweet I can handle.
MEMORIAL TRACKERS
MEMORIAL TRACKERS

Track team

After winning the regional cross country meet in the fall, the Memorial Middle School team started the track season off on a great foot! Even our field event star, Tom Rawson (below) felt brave enough to try a track event.

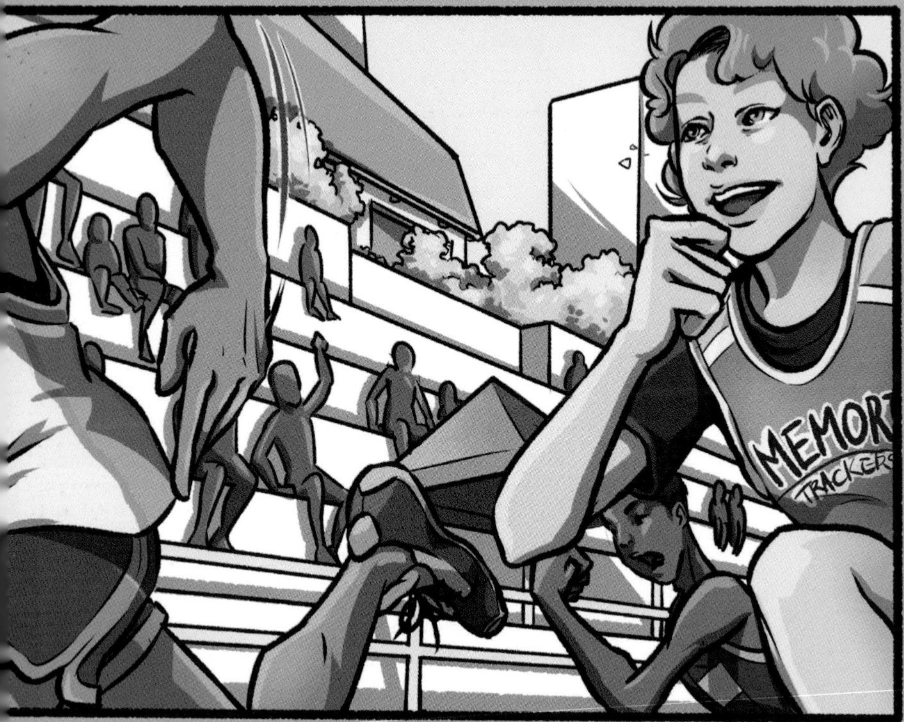

MEMORI
TRACKERS

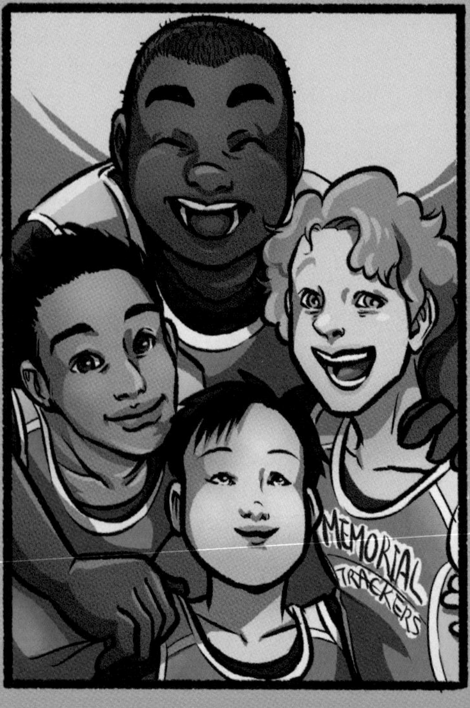

MEMORIAL
TRACKERS

Our boys 4x400 team of (from top) De'Andre Harrison, Jack Bennet, Tom Rawson, and David Yu can't be beat!

Runner Allie Chaing (right) stretches before making her next record-breaking laps.

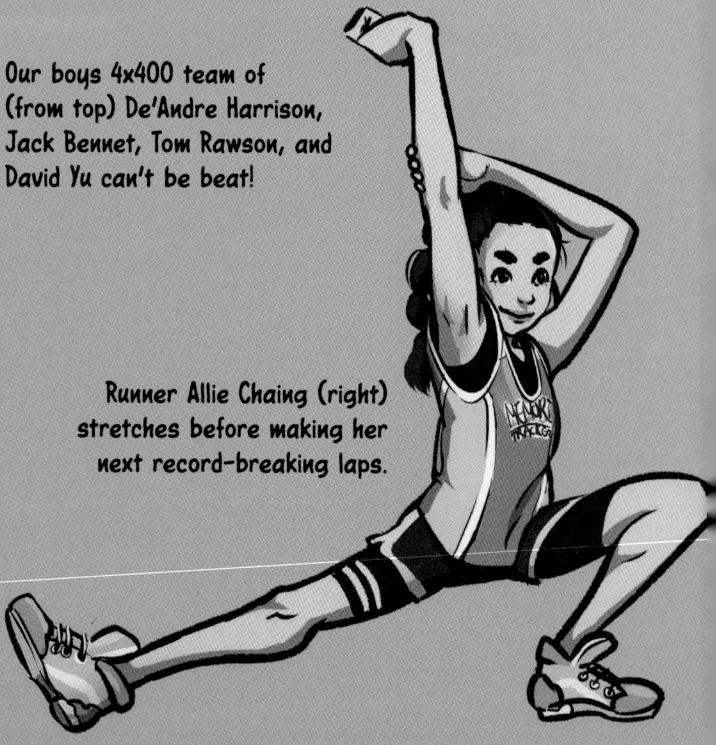

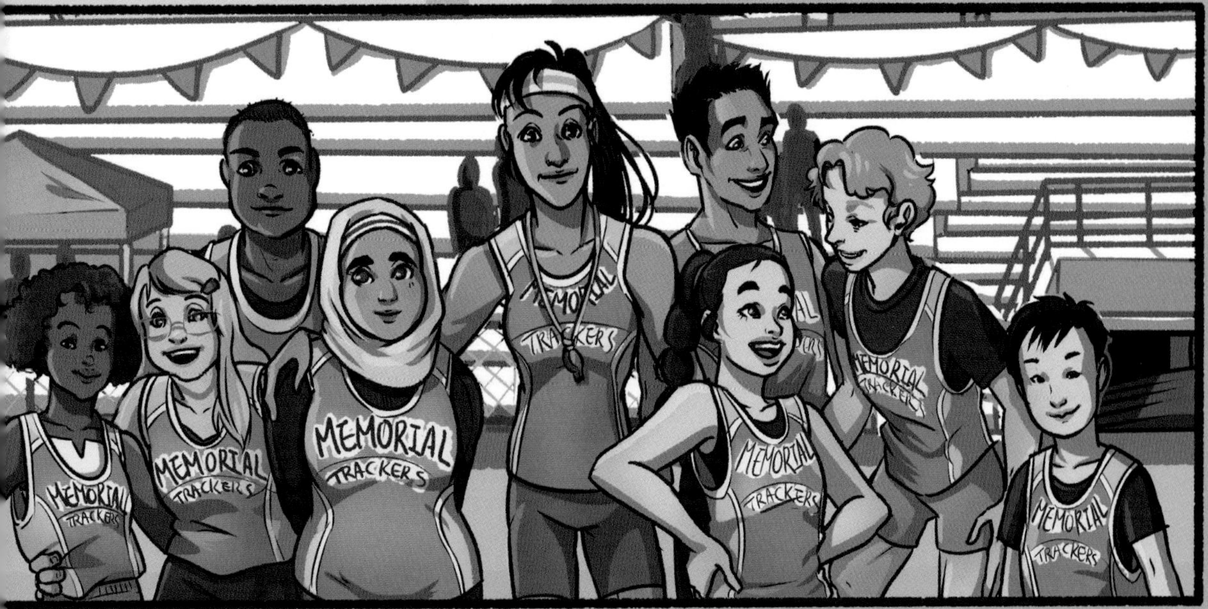
MEMORIAL
TRACKERS

Coach Ortiz is such an inspiration to the team! Our 4x400 teams (above) have never been faster.

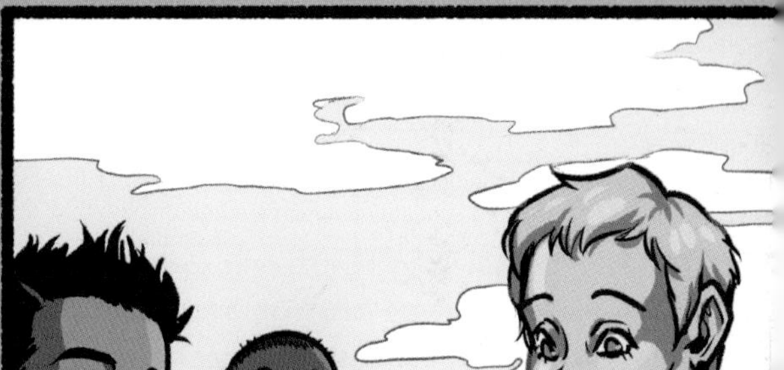
MEMORIAL
TRACKERS

Lifelong friendships are formed on the track team. Vi Bronson (below, left) and Tami Conley (below, right) became best friends after meeting at practice.

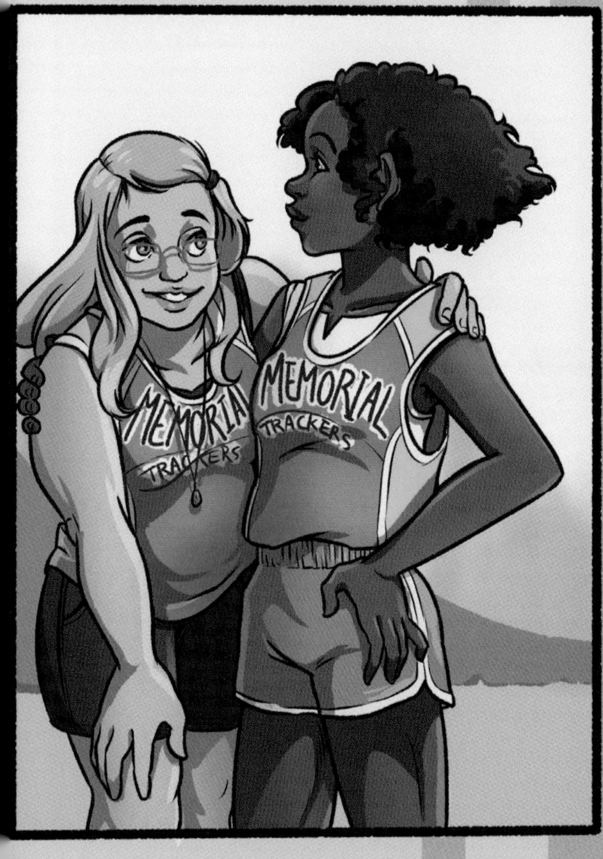
MEMORIAL
TRACKERS

Allie Chaing (above) convinced Ms. Davidson at Dozen Donut to make sugar-free breakfast cookies for the entire track team. They're the perfect treat for away meets!

Track team Bake Sale!

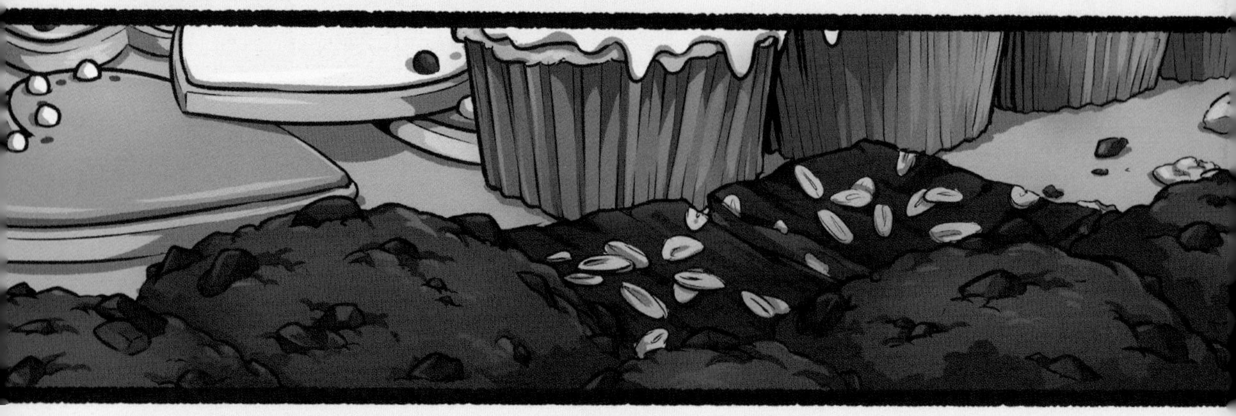

The track team needed new timing equipment, so we kicked our fundraising efforts into high gear! Everyone baked, glazed, frosted, and decorated their family's favorites for this weeklong food and fun fundraiser.

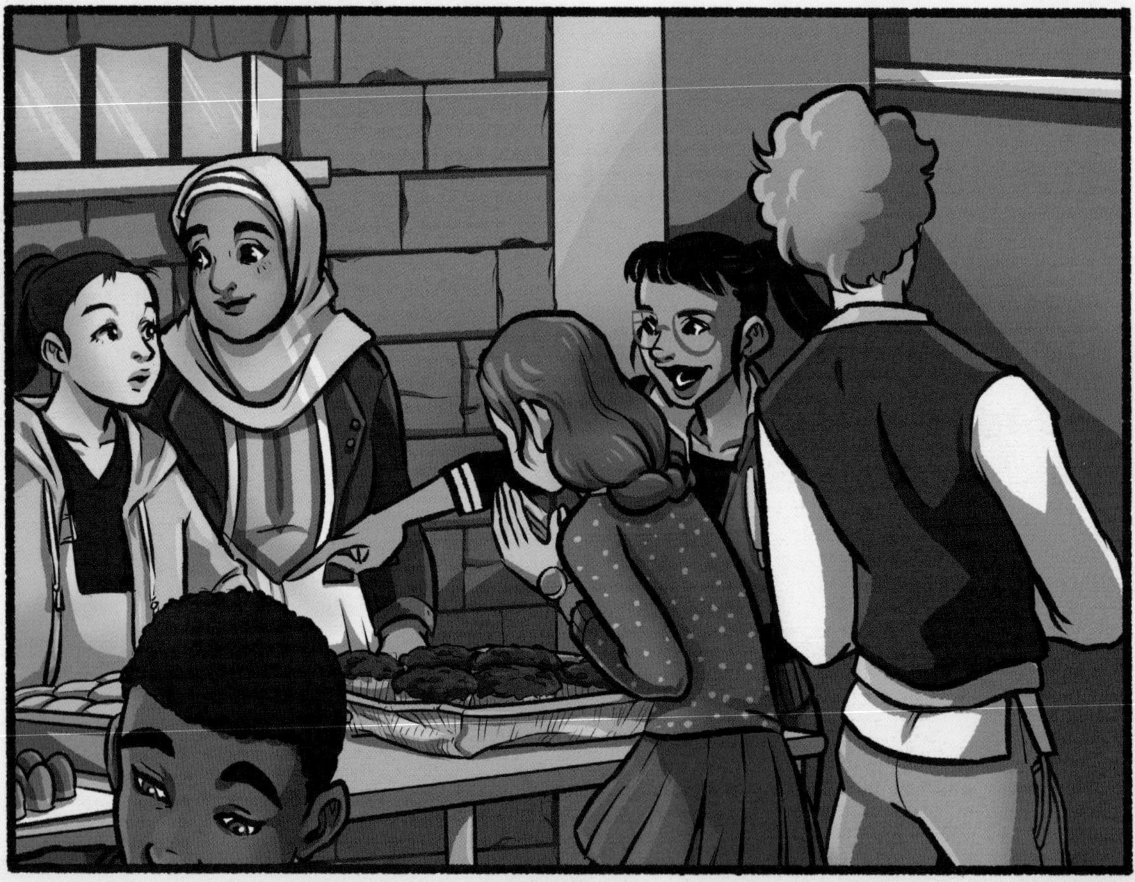

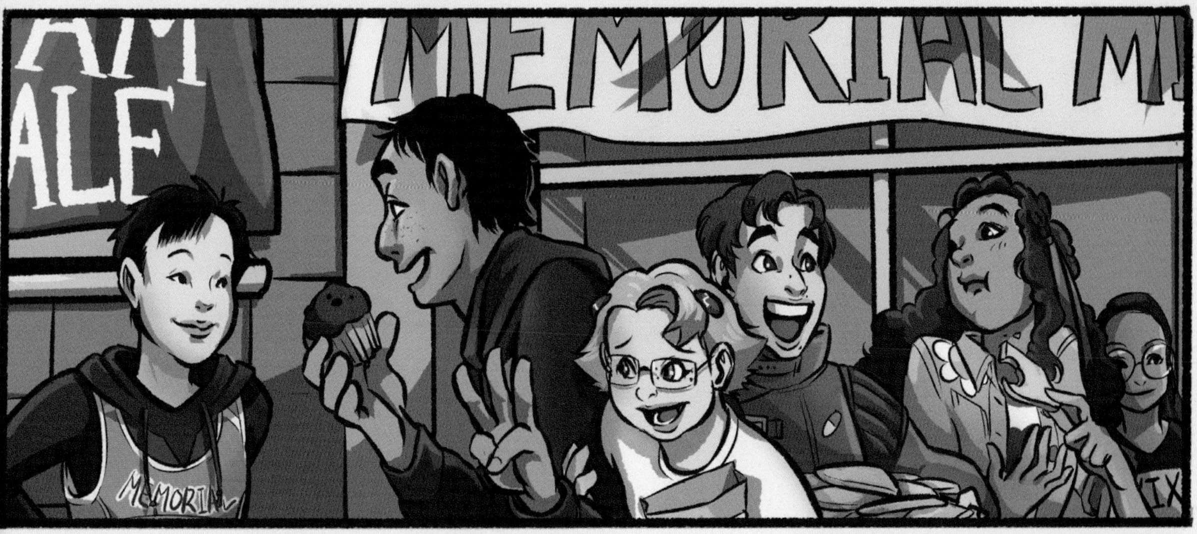
MEMORIAL
MEMORIAL

The Anime Club is always up for a tasty treat! (From left: David Yu, Austin Cooper, Franny Luca, Scooter deJesus, Lilly Rodriguez, and Jenny Book)

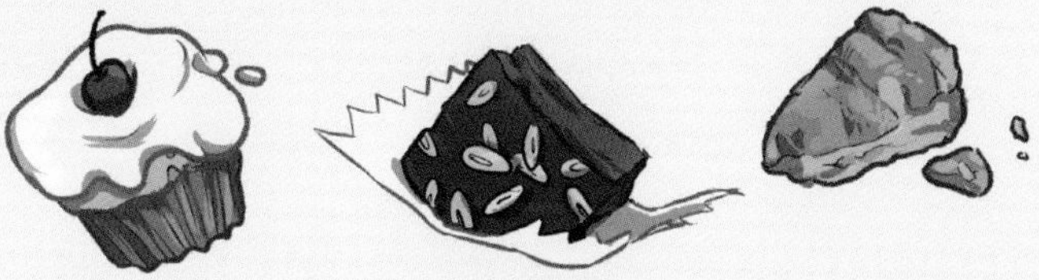

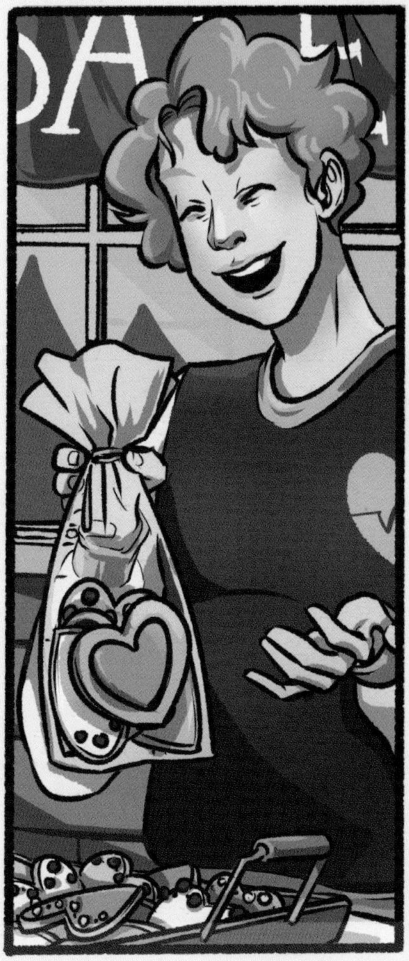

Tom Rawson (right) has a sister who is in culinary school. She made us some great sugar cookies!

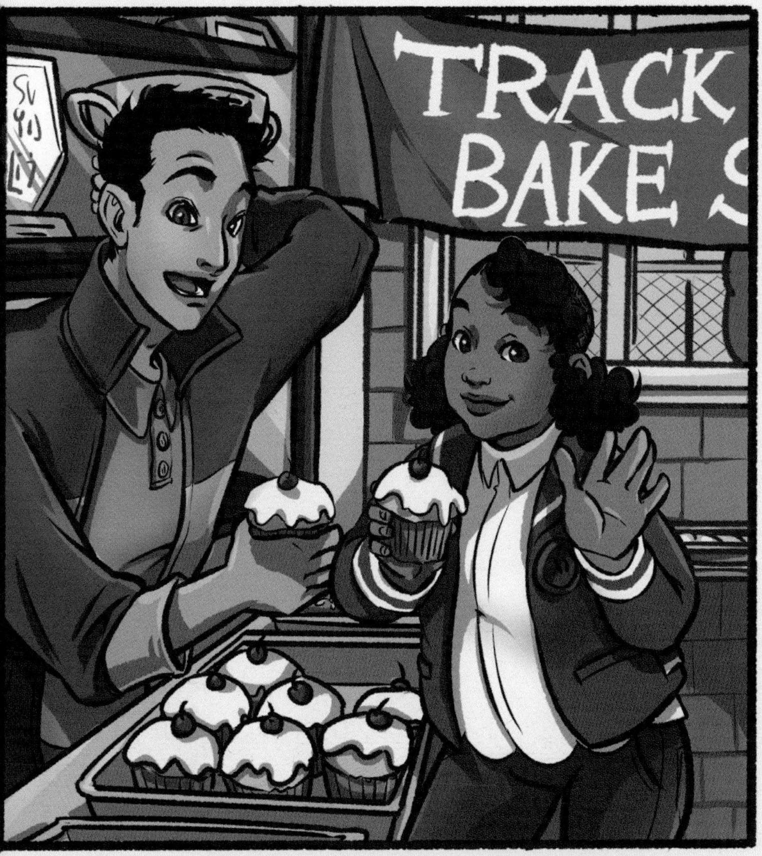
TRACK
BAKE

Jack Bennet (left) and Kamilla Davis (right) met on the track. You can join them every Tuesday and Thursday morning for Get Fit/Fab Club.

LIVING WITH DIABETES

TYPE 1 DIABETES	**TYPE 2 DIABETES**
The body doesn't make enough insulin	Body can't use insulin properly
Can develop at any age	Can develop at any age
No known way to prevent it	Most cases are preventable
About **5%** of those diagnosed with diabetes have type 1	**1** out of **3** people will develop type 2 diabetes

More than **30 million** American children and adults have diabetes.

But **1** in **4** don't know it!

GET TESTED! WORK WITH A DOCTOR

EAT SMART!
COUNT YOUR CARBS

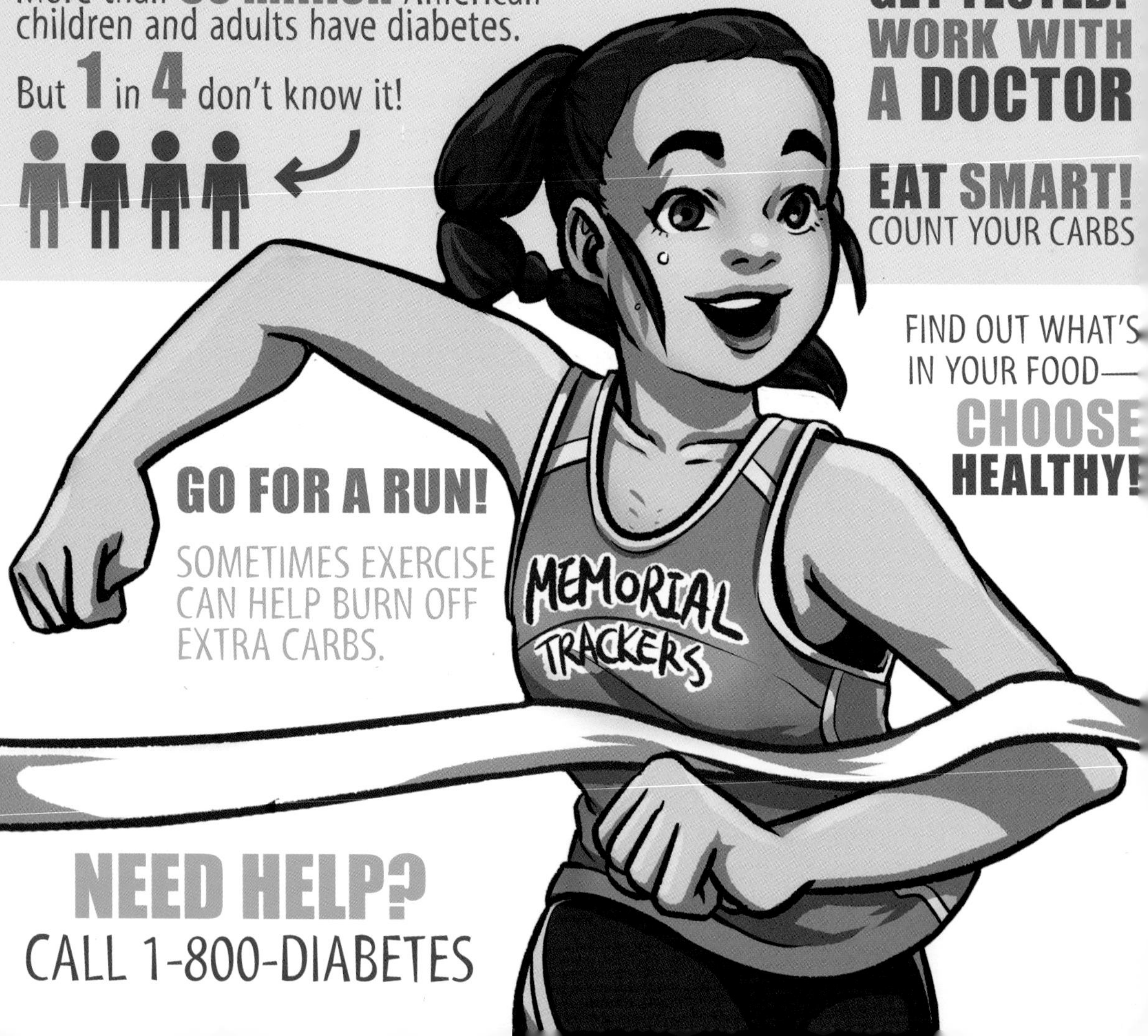
MEMORIAL
TRACKERS

FIND OUT WHAT'S IN YOUR FOOD—
CHOOSE HEALTHY!

GO FOR A RUN!

SOMETIMES EXERCISE CAN HELP BURN OFF EXTRA CARBS.

NEED HELP?
CALL 1-800-DIABETES

ALLIE INTERVIEWS
NURSE CAROL

ALLIE: Hi Nurse Carol! Thanks for squeezing me in! Track practice has been crazy. Sections, here we come!

NURSE CAROL: I'm so excited for the team! And I'm glad you're working so hard, both on the field and off. How have things been at home?

ALLIE: Great! But I was hoping you'd be able to offer some advice for families with teens who are living with diabetes.

NURSE CAROL: Absolutely! It's hard enough being a teenager the way it is. But when you add diabetes to the mix, things can get even tougher.

ALLIE: What do you think the first step should be?

NURSE CAROL: The most important thing for parents, I think, is to focus on communication. Parents should ask and aswer questions honestly. And everyone should make decisions and set realistic goals when it comes to lifestyle changes.

ALLIE: I know my mom had a lot of concerns. Maybe too many!

NURSE CAROL: Just remember, they're concerned because they care. Put yourselves in each others' shoes. It's a big change, for everyone. If the whole family is on the same page, glucose checks, diet, and exercise will be a little easier to manage together.

ALLIE: That's true. Things have gotten much better at home since I sat down and told my mom and dad what was going on.

NURSE CAROL: And a huge thing to remember is that diabetes is a lifelong condition—but manageable with proper care. Be sure you have all the information you need to manage your health, and speak up when you're not feeling well. Self-care is important! But don't let diabetes stop you from reaching your goals. Make sure they're realistic, and celebrate even small victories.

ALLIE: Like the state track title! Thanks for all the great advice, Nurse Carol.

GLOSSARY

ANOREXIA — eating disorder characterized by extreme weight loss

AUTOIMMUNE DISEASE — a disease in which the body mistakenly produces proteins called antibodies that attack its own tissues

CARBOHYDRATE — a substance found in foods such as bread, rice, cereal, and potatoes that gives you energy

DIABETES — a disease in which there is too much sugar in the blood

GENETICS — relating to physical traits or conditions passed down from parents to children

GLUCOSE — a natural sugar found in plants that gives energy to living things

HYPOGLYCEMIA — the medical term for low blood sugar

INSULIN — a substance made in the pancreas that helps the body use sugar

SYRINGE — a tube with a plunger and a hollow needle; licensed practical nurses use syringes to inject medicine into patients

QUESTIONS

1. What do you know about diabetes? Find two or three websites about diabetes, and write down at least five facts.

2. Living with diabetes forces Allie to make some big changes. What are they? Using the information you gathered, explain why you think they were necessary or useful.

3. On pages 33–34, some of Allie's classmates make an assumption about her health. How could they have handled the situation differently?

CHALLENGE!

Have you ever heard a rumor being spread about someone you know? Shut it down! Calmly ask the person spreading the rumor to stop spreading it. It can be hard to stand up to a bully. But it can be even harder for the person being gossiped about.